Moskov Selim

GEORGIOS VIZYENOS

Moskov Selim

Translated by
Peter Mackridge

AIORA

Peter Mackridge is Emeritus Professor of Modern Greek at the University of Oxford. He has published several books on modern Greek language and literature, including two co-authored grammars. His most recent translations are *Thracian Tales* by Vizyenos and a story by the 19th-century author Alexandros Papadiamandis (both 2014), and *The History of Western Philosophy in 100 Haiku* by the 21st-century poet Haris Vlavianos (2015).

Original title: *Ο Μοσκώβ Σελήμ*

© Aiora Press 2015

Reprinted March 2022

ISBN: 978-618-5048-27-3

AIORA PRESS
11 Mavromichali st.
Athens 10679 - Greece
tel: +30 210 3839000
www.aiorabooks.com

Contents

Introduction 9

Moskov Selim 23

Chronological outline... 91

Introduction

Thrace is a corner of south-east Europe where Greece, Bulgaria and Turkey meet. The Greek writer Georgios (George) Vizyenos was born there in 1849. As a child he was simply called "Mick's son Georgie", but as an adult he adopted the surname by which he became known as a writer. "Vizyenos" means "the man from Vizye", after the small town in Thrace where he was born and spent his early years. Vizye (Vize in Turkish) is situated between Constantinople (Istanbul), about 85 miles to the south-east, and Adrianople (Edirne), which today is near the border with Bulgaria. Vizye was then, and still is today, in Turkey, but in those days it had a sizeable Greek population, as did Constantinople, which was the capital of the Ottoman empire.

Vizyenos had a curious life and career. His father, a pedlar, died when George was five years old; two of his sisters perished in early childhood; and one of his brothers died in mysterious circumstances. So as not to be a burden to his widowed mother, and so as to supplement the family's meagre income, George left home at the age of ten to be apprenticed to a tailor in Istanbul. After following this trade for eight years he was singled out by a succession of rich Greek patrons who were struck by his exceptional intellectual talents and decided to encourage them. He began studying for the priesthood, but he abandoned this vocation and at the age of twenty-four he entered high school in Athens and in the same year published his first book of poetry and completed his second.

After spending a year at school, he entered Athens University, but he became dissatisfied with his studies there and in 1875 he went to Germany, where he completed his education at the universities of Göttingen, Leipzig and Berlin—still supported by rich patrons—with a dissertation on the psychology of children's play. After a further period of study in London and Paris, Vizyenos returned to Greece with the aim of becoming a university lecturer in the history of philosophy. However, he failed to fulfil this ambition and instead taught in high schools until 1890, when he was appointed Professor of Drama at the Athens Conservatoire.

By this time Vizyenos had established himself as a poet and fiction-writer, but he was made to feel an outsider in the literary and academic world of Athens. The tragedies and privations of his early life, his extraordinary rise from tailor's assistant to doctor of philosophy, and the professional and personal difficulties he encountered on the way led to grave mental instability, and, one day in

1892, having conceived a passion for a teenage girl, he was found dressed as a bridegroom and claiming that he was about to marry her. He spent the last four years of his life in Daphni mental asylum, where he died in 1896.

Vizyenos' prose work consists of six long stories, of which the first five appeared in the Athens magazine *Estia* in 1883 and 1884. His first story, "My mother's sin", was one of the earliest examples of the genre to be published in Greece.

MOSKOV SELIM

"Moskov Selim" was the last story Vizyenos wrote. Whereas the three stories included in the volume I entitled *Thracian Tales* (published by Aiora in 2014) appeared in 1883-4, "Moskov Selim" was written in 1886 or 1887 and appeared in *Estia* in 1895, just a year before the author's death. Most of the plot of "Moskov Selim" takes place in Thrace (the nearby town of V., with its Byzantine walls and towers, is clearly reminiscent of Vizyenos' birthplace), but unlike the other Thracian tales its chief character is not a member of the narrator's family, nor is there any reference to the narrator's childhood. It is also longer than any of the earlier Thracian tales.

Moskov Selim, the name by which the hero is known to his neighbours, is almost a contradiction in terms. It means, in Turkish, "Moscow Selim" or "Selim from Moscow", as we might say "Glasgow Joe" or "Chicago Pete". In those days a Turk from Russia would have been considered an impossibility, since the Turks and the Russians had been fighting each other, off and on, for three hundred years. Indeed, during the previous two centuries there had been Russo-Turkish wars in 1676-81, 1686-1700, 1710-11, 1735-39, 1768-74, 1787-92, 1806-12, 1828-29, 1853-56 (the Crimean War) and, most recently, 1877-78. Because of this, it seemed natural at the time that every Turk was an implacable enemy of every Russian, and vice versa.

In Vizyenos' lifetime Thrace was inhabited by Greeks, Turks and Bulgarians and it formed part of the Ottoman empire, whose capital was Constantinople (Istanbul). When Vizyenos was writing it had become obvious that the Ottoman empire, especially as far as its European possessions were concerned, had not long to live. The first great blow against the Empire by one of its subject peoples had been struck by the Greeks during their successful War of Independence in the 1820s. Although the new Greek state covered a mere fraction of the total territory that Greece's political and intellectual leaders hoped to gain, this war acted as an inspiration to the Greeks and other non-Muslims still living under Ottoman rule, giving them hope that they too would soon be liberated.

By the time Vizyenos wrote "Moskov Selim" in the late 1880s, Ottoman territory in Europe had been drastically reduced, chiefly as a result of the Russo-Turkish war of 1877-78: Serbia and Romania had become fully independent of the Ottoman empire, an autonomous principality of Bulgaria had been established with its capital at Sofia,

Bosnia-Herzegovina had revolted and been subsequently occupied by Austro-Hungary, and Greece had annexed a portion of Thessaly and Epirus. Meanwhile other liberation movements were taking place, particularly in Crete. But throughout the nineteenth century the chief threat to the Ottoman empire appeared to be posed by Russia, which was seeking to increase its influence in south-east Europe and was perceived by the Turks as being behind the various revolutionary movements there.

Three of the Russo-Turkish wars that took place during the nineteenth century are referred to in "Moskov Selim". Pavloshka's father had taken part in the 1828-29 war, while Selim himself fought in the Crimean War and the war of 1877-78. The chief event in the Crimean War that Selim mentions is the siege of Silistra on the Bulgarian side of the Danube, which the Turks were obliged to relinquish to Bulgaria twenty-four years later. The 1877-78 war serves as the backdrop to much of the action of Vizyenos' story "Who was my brother's murderer?"; the chief event in this war mentioned by Selim is the five-month Russian and Romanian siege of Plevna in northern Bulgaria, which resulted in the capture of that strategic town by Turkey's enemies. The British historian A. J. P. Taylor wrote that "Plevna is one of the few engagements which changed the course of history".[1] Vizyenos, through the mouth of Selim, focuses on the sufferings of

1. A.J.P. Taylor, *The Struggle for Mastery in Europe 1848-1918* (Oxford 1954), p. 245.

the Ottoman troops while they were defending the city and particularly during their attempts to evade capture. In addition, Selim had previously volunteered to help put down a revolt in Herzegovina in 1861-62 and, at the age of forty, had taken part, again as a volunteer, in the war between Turkey and Serbia in 1876; in this context he refers to the Turkish capture of Aleksinac on the River Morava.

The long decline of the Ottoman empire lasted from the 1680s, when it was at the height of its power, until 1922, when the sultanate was formally abolished. All the events mentioned in the previous paragraph form part of the long-drawn-out "solution" to what was known in Europe from the late eighteenth century onwards as the Eastern Question. This was the question of how and when the Ottoman empire would come to an end and how its territories would be divided out among its neighbours. Many of the Greek political and intellectual leaders of Vizyenos' time were hoping that Greece would gain substantial advantages from all this turmoil in the Balkans, and some of them even dreamed of recapturing Constantinople from the Sultan. Indeed, in 1913, seventeen years after Vizyenos' death, Greece's position as one of the victors in the Balkan Wars against the Ottoman empire ensured that it was granted huge amounts of Ottoman territory. However, Greece's defeat at the end of the Greco-Turkish war in 1922 prevented it from gaining further territory from the Turks, and in fact all of the one and half million Greeks living in Turkey—including the

Greek inhabitants of Vizyenos' native town—were expelled to Greece, deprived forever of the right to return to their homes. In this way, what the narrator of "Moskov Selim" calls the "Byzantine hope"—the fantasy that the Turks would retreat from Europe and hand Constantinople back to the Greeks—was violently shattered forever.

A contemporary resonance can be heard in a sentence used by the narrator towards the end of his story: "Is it to be wondered, then, that a man such as Moskov Selim should feel that the fated hour has now come when the Caliph must transfer his throne to Damascus or Baghdad?" For many centuries until the Ottoman capture of Constantinople from the Byzantines in 1453, the capital of the Islamic caliphate (the word "caliph" means successor to the Prophet Muhammed) had been Baghdad. From 1453 onwards, however, the Ottoman sultans claimed to be the caliphs, which meant that they saw themselves as the rulers of the Muslim world. When the Ottoman empire and the Sultanate were abolished by the Turkish Republic in 1922, the caliphate was abolished with them. As of 2014, efforts are being made to re-establish the caliphate in Iraq and Syria.

As in Vizyenos' earlier Thracian tales, much of "Moskov Selim" is taken up by the central character telling his own story. The experiences narrated by the characters in the earlier stories go a long way towards elucidating the enigmas posed in the titles (what was the one and only journey of whose life? what was the mother's sin? who was the brother's murderer?). In the same way, in this last of Vizyenos' Thracian tales Selim's own narrative explains how this Turkish Muslim came to be known as "the Muscovite". When the narrator expresses his surprise at the Turk's desire to be a prisoner of the Russians again, Selim explains: "It seems strange to you because you don't know my story." As is the case with the earlier stories, Selim's narration of his life story is a cathartic and therapeutic act that relieves him of the burden of pent-up knowledge. Again, the narrator plays a crucial role in this process, not only as the person who elicits the character's life story in the first place but also as the person who relays it to the reader ("If you tell your troubles to him, it's like telling the whole world," as Selim puts it).

The relation between the narrator and the other characters in "Moskov Selim" is strikingly different from the situation in the three earlier Thracian tales. In those previous stories most of the other characters are members of the narrator's family (his mother, his grandparents and his two brothers), and the narrator's psychological disturbance at the revelation of the characters' hitherto secret stories is due to the fact that, since these stories chiefly concern his nearest and dearest, they also ultimately concern himself: he comes to realize that his own life is intimately bound up with often traumatic experiences which hitherto he has been unaware of.

In "Moskov Selim" the relationship is different, since the narrator has never met the chief character before, the two men are not connected by kinship or longstanding mutual friendship, and they have spent their previous lives in quite different places. In the earlier stories the narrator is forced to reassess his childhood in the light of what he learns much later, whereas here the narrator's past is not overtly mentioned at all. The disturbing relationship in this case is not one of kinship, but of similarity. A photograph of Vizyenos shows him posing against a painted backdrop of rocks, trees and bracken. In this photograph, taken in Germany in 1879, he is wearing a thick woollen jacket buttoned up to the neck, trousers,

and high boots that come up to his knees. His moustache and beard are thick but trimmed, and he wears a tall brimless hat, slightly tapering towards the crown, that looks like the kind of fez worn by Ottoman gentlemen of the time, including Sultan Abdul Hamid II himself. Yet, in "Moskov Selim", the narrator's fur hat and boots lead Selim to mistake him for a Russian. To cap the irony, Selim too is wearing high boots and a fez. Thus Vizyenos and Selim are both depicted wearing a mixture of oriental, Russian and western dress.

In "Who was my brother's murderer?" the narrator initially expresses a conventional Greek distaste for the Turks, but gradually, through personal contact with individual Turkish characters, he comes to sympathize with their plight. His initial attitude, born of ignorance and prejudice, is radically modified by experience. A similar process is depicted in "Moskov Selim", but here the experience is doubled. The Turk Selim had come to see, on close acquaintance with Russians, that the nation he had hated so fiercely consisted of kind-hearted, hospitable individuals who behaved with compassion towards the unfortunate enemy prisoners of war they found in their midst. Similarly, the narrator gradually begins to feel compassion for Selim, seeing him not as a representative of his race and religion, but as a suffering individual, whose life experiences have placed him in a position not so different from his own. Selim feels that he had been rejected by his family as a child, that he is despised and ridiculed by his neighbours in the present, and that the best days of his life were the time he spent in Russia. Similarly, if we identify the narrator with Vizyenos himself, we see someone who had spent a traumatic childhood and as an adult was marginalized as a writer and scholar in Athens, and who perhaps viewed his years of education in Germany and elsewhere in western Europe as the happiest and most fulfilling period of his life. Selim belongs neither to the Turks nor to the Russians, just as the author feels alienated from and rejected by his own people without having become integrated into western European culture. Thus Selim is perhaps as much a symbolic representation of the author as the narrator is his more realistic *alter ego*. At one point the narrator writes: "My companion's description of Moskov Selim as crazy now seemed to me to be an insult against myself." And later on he tells us that he feels a "correspondence of souls" between him and Selim.

The confusion concerning national identity and national allegiance in "Moskov Selim" is connected to an uncertainty about sexual identity. It cannot be a coincidence that the chief characters in two of Vizyenos' stories are men who have spent some of their childhood being raised as girls: the grandfather in "The one and only journey of his life" is dressed as a girl until the eve of his marriage at the age of ten in order to save him from the Ottoman officials who toured the Christian areas of the Empire press-ganging unmarried boys into the janissaries, while Selim, the youngest of three brothers, is brought up as a girl until the age of twelve because his mother "wanted to fool herself and console herself for not having a daughter"—with the result that he is despised and rejected by the father he so admires. One cannot help associating these situations with the fact that in "My mother's sin" the willingness of the narrator's mother to let him die in order to save her daughter suggests that she wishes she had given birth to a girl instead of a boy—an unusual wish in traditional Greek culture, but one that is understandable in the exceptional circumstances of that particular story.

Selim, like the grandfather in "The one and only journey of his life", is something of a fantasist. Selim's conception of Russia as being an ideal country, a promised land, plays a similar symbolic role to the imaginary places the grandfather expects his grandson to have travelled to: the sea's belly-button, the land where the dog people live, and the land where the sun bakes the bread. When the boy narrator, who has been living in Constantinople, tells the old man he hasn't seen any of these places, the grandfather tells him that in that case he hasn't seen anything. Similarly, when the much-travelled narrator tells him he has never visited Russia, Selim tells him, "Well, then, you haven't been anywhere."

In "Moskov Selim", through the mouth of the narrator and without renouncing his allegiance to Hellenism and Christianity, Vizyenos expresses his belief in the possibility of a symbiosis and mutual understanding, on a personal level, between Greek and Turk, Christian and Muslim. Nonetheless, despite the narrator's comment that there were "reasons of political expediency" behind the care lavished by the Russians on their prisoners-of-war, one can't help noticing that Vizyenos depicts Christianity trumping Islam because of the compassion displayed by the Russians towards Selim, in contrast to the callousness and indifference with which the Turks in authority behave towards him. At the end of the story, however, blood proves to be thicker than water: despite having outwardly rejected his "national character", at a time of mortal danger Selim comes to a final realization of where his innermost allegiance lies.

Moskov Selim

Would that you had never crossed my path! Would that I had never met you! You good, strange Turk, you filled my heart with sorrow, as if the grief caused every single day by the fate of my compatriots were not enough!

But what has passed has passed. Your lean, sorrowful face with its melancholy, penetrating gaze disturbs my sleep and haunts my solitude. Your trembling, doleful voice rings plaintively in my ears. I need to write your story.

I have no doubt that the fanatics among your people will revile the memory of one of the faithful for opening the innermost recesses of his heart to the profane eyes of an infidel. I fear too that the fanatics among my own people may find fault with a Greek writer for not concealing your virtues, or else for not replacing you by a Christian hero in your narrative. No matter: that will in no way detract from your merit in confiding your life's adventures to me; and my conscience will never be troubled because, as a simple chronicler, I valued in you not the implacable enemy of my nation, but simply the man. So, no matter: I shall write your story.

The summer was almost past; it was towards evening. After ten hours' ride through largely waterless villages we reached V., the seat of the local administration in eastern Thrace. On the lofty acropolis we could already discern the black shapes of the fallen Byzantine towers, while above the red-roofed houses the two or three minarets of the market town rose erect, whitened by the bright light of the peacefully setting sun. In order to reach the end of our journey we had to ride only a few kilometres further, but we had first to water the horses so that they could digest, as the local people put it, before they reached the stable.

"Shall we water here?" I asked my companion when I espied a small stream flowing by in front of us.

"No, let's water at Kaynardja, a little further on. It's not quite on our way, but after all this exertion you deserve to be introduced to Kaynardja. It's the water of immortality—it bubbles up from inside the rock."

After a while we turned off the road, and passing through a series of hills which were mostly tree-covered but were all, without exception, picturesque, we reached the place to which my companion insisted on introducing me.

Kaynardja indeed presents a most delightful spectacle, owing its Turkish name to the fact that the gushing
spring gives the impression of a seething cauldron. Its
ice-cold waters, as clear as liquid diamonds might be,
pour sparkling from the depths of a white wall of lime-
stone with a charmingly mysterious whisper, as thick
and fast and untiring as though they were waves of
magical life-giving subterranean liquors which the
Earth, that queenly Mother, sends forth from her bo-
som with limitless bounty to flow throughout the broad
plain and nourish the profusion of flowers and other
plants that would otherwise languish under the deadly
shafts of the summer sun.

Along this purling blue water-course there flour-
ished a sizeable verdant oasis, forming a level terrain
from which there emerged green reeds and bulrushes,
a favourite haunt of the "fair-winged damsel" and many
other flying insects of various shapes and sizes. Clumps
of wild willows, with squat trunks and dense branches,
offered an evening refuge to a flock of turtle-doves. The
evening breeze brought their sweet love-plaints to our
ears, while a rapacious hawk, stationed high up on the
dead branch of a lightning-struck plane-tree, lay in wait
for the blithe, limpid-voiced larks which, invisible in the
heights of the ether, scattered the day's last song.

The boundless fields surrounding this oasis had by
now yielded up their treasures to the threshing floors of
the nearby villages, and consequently the countryside,

as far as the eye could see, was deserted and desolate. Only the shepherds' flutes could be heard in the distance, summoning the flocks into the pens for the evening milking.

The burning heat of the day was still intense; and, since the water that springs forth from the northern slopes builds up in the marshy ground at the eastern end of the huge plain, the mist that usually rises in the morning and evening began to cover the bare expanses towards the horizon, merging the sky in that direction with the earth.

When, having drunk and washed at the cooling spring, I ran my gaze over the landscape, I thought I had suddenly been transported to some oasis in the steppes of southern Russia. A little house, built some way from the spring on a hillock and scarcely visible behind the thick foliage of two tall beeches, contributed wondrously to the enhancement of this illusion. This little house, constructed entirely of wood, was clearly an imitation of that mean type of dwelling that the Russian peasants call *izba*. Even the chimney-stack of such houses is made of roughly hewn pieces of wood; and at that moment wisps of white smoke were rising from it and curling around the foliage of the trees.

"Who lives there?" I asked my companion, who was a native of these parts.

"Moskov Selim," he replied casually.

"Is he a Russian who stayed behind after the last war?"

"On the contrary, he's a local Turk. He was taken to Russia as a prisoner-of-war, but he didn't do us the favour of staying behind—he's got nine lives!"

"How do you mean, nine lives?"

"Well, he's been knocked about in the wars for twenty-five years, and the ravens have never come to take his carcass away."

"And what does he do now?"

"He cultivates that little garden and sells his produce—he has a cow and some hens too. He also sells cups of tea. He's a crazy fellow."

"How can he be crazy," I retorted, "if he lives so sensibly?"

"But he is. Why do you think he's called Moskov Selim? He's crazy about the Russians. At first the Turks tried to get him out of the way because they saw him as a traitor. Then they realized he was a bit weak in the head, so they let him be. He wants nothing to do with them: he's waiting for the Russians, he says, and that's all. The Turks come here, they eat and drink, make fun of him and amuse themselves at his expense."

But before he could finish his sentence, he exclaimed: "There he is! That's Moskov Selim that I'm talking about. He's seen you in your fur hat and your boots—he's bound to have taken you for a Russian. You don't know how impatient he is for the Russians to come—that's why people tease him and make fun of him."

Indeed, a man appeared, tall and erect, walking towards us from the house with firm strides. He looked well past middle age. Despite the dryness of the terrain, his long legs were sunk up to the thighs in high military boots such as the Cossacks had sold by the ten thousand to the local inhabitants during their withdrawal from Thrace. Was it that they loved the area so much that, since their feet were no longer permitted to tread this sacred soil, they left their boots behind instead? Or was it that they loved money so much that they preferred to return home from Turkey with lighter feet and heavier purses? I do not know. What is certain is that Moskov Selim's boots could no longer act as the representatives of Russian feet on Thracian soil, for their soles had become so worn that the Russian leather had long since been supplanted by the soles of Moskov Selim's own feet.

By way of contrast the Turk wore round his middle a bright red oriental cummerbund whose innumerable folds, like layers of swaddling-bands, covered and distorted his torso from groin to chest. This rendered Moskov Selim's bearing all the more comical, since the garment which he wore over his sash and his shirt was plainly an old army greatcoat with two or three carefully polished Russian buttons and with traces of faded stripes on its collar and sleeves. Moskov Selim wore on his head, for good measure, the tall fez of a Turkish soldier, but without a tassel, held on by a fine green

kerchief wound round his temples. A more bizarre out-
fit could not be imagined, even by those local people
who have ridiculous pretentions to fashion.

"*Dobro doiti, bratushka*! (Welcome, brother!)," exclaimed the Turk in obvious excitement as he ap-
proached. Then, as I returned his greeting in the Turkish
manner, he brought his heels together and, assuming
a warlike posture, saluted like a Russian soldier.

"How do you do?" I said. "Are you well?"

"Miserable," he replied, "thank God!"

Putting out his bony hand, he grasped mine and
shook it vehemently. Then he leaned towards my ear
and enquired in a low voice and, as I realized, with
tender familiarity:

"*Moskov? Moskov?*"

I stared at him uncomprehendingly, but he winked
and made an expressive gesture, as if to say, "Don't you
worry! Even though you won't admit it in front of this
third party, I can tell you're a Russian and I'm glad of it."

"Not *Moskov!*" I replied in embarrassment. "Not
Moskov! Christian, *Rum.*"

Moskov Selim's expectations having now been cruelly deceived, his tall stature sagged at every joint, so
that from that moment he became at least a hand's
breadth shorter.

Moskov Selim must have been more than forty years
old, but his bearing and his black hair made him look
younger. Whereas the rest of his body was very lean, he

had a well developed head and a regularly protruding brow; but the flesh on his face looked unnaturally pale and flaccid. It was as if he had just recovered from a long illness. His languid, tremulous voice and his look of deep melancholy made a contrast with his manly bearing. His large eyes, crowned by thick, regularly curving eyebrows, were especially endearing.

It is strange how some faces, hitherto unknown to us, have the power to seize our imagination from their first appearance without our knowing through what cause and for what purpose. Such was the effect that Moskov Selim's appearance had on me. It seized my sympathy and interest as if by storm, in spite of his comic costume. While my companion led the horses about by the bridle so that they would recover their breath from the journey before they drank, I attempted to find out from Selim whether it was poverty or some other reason that made him reside there and made him feel, as he put it, "miserable". But he craftily avoided any explanation, inviting me to have coffee and asking me where I was from and whether I knew about any new Russian expedition to Turkey. I was quite willing to sip my coffee by the gushing streams of Kaynardja, but, as for the Russians, I had nothing to reply that would have pleased my host.

I managed somehow to avoid this pitfall by counter-attacking with a series of questions. To each of these he responded with such apt brevity as further to intensify, rather than satisfy, my curiosity to learn his story. I had become convinced about one thing in his respect, namely that the incongruity of his dress bore no relation to the world of his ideas. My companion's description of Moskov Selim as crazy now seemed to me to be an insult against myself. The only strange thing about the man was that his appraisal of certain matters was somewhat unexpected.

"Have you travelled to many parts?" he asked as I prepared to mount my horse. "Have you been to Russia?"

"Russia's the only place I haven't been," I replied playfully.

"Well, then, you haven't been anywhere—that's why you've travelled to all those places and come back again. If you should once go to Russia, you'll find you won't have the heart to leave."

"How's that?" I asked with a smile.

"We can't talk now," he replied. "You've watered the horses and you mustn't keep them waiting—you must ride them and squeeze their fat a bit so they'll digest their water."

We mounted and spurred the horses, and I did not exchange a word with my companion until we reached our lodgings. My imagination was completely taken up by the Turk. I wished to spend a little time in the town of V. by way of refreshment and relaxation from work that had long occupied my mind so fully that I could find no respite even in sleep. Knowing this, my hosts withdrew immediately after dinner on the reasonable pretext that, weary as I was from the long ride, I needed to rest. In this they were not mistaken, but—who would have believed it?—it was precisely that night, during which I had hoped to have my fill of sleep, that I was to pass in complete sleeplessness.

The appearance of the Turk next to Kaynardja with his bizarre dress and his Russian house—which would have been so insignificant, even ridiculous, in any other circumstances—gained such a hold on my imagination that night that quite unwillingly I counted the long nocturnal hours making all sorts of surmises and drawing various conclusions about that appealing, melancholy and at the same time curiously manly character. He was certainly not crazy, I told myself. Nor was he some unfortunate creature in whom insanity was already adumbrated in his obsessively pro-Russian sentiments. A mysterious shadow, betrayed in his dreamy, melancholy eyes, seemed to possess his inner self.

But what clarity there was in his speech, what dignity in his bearing! In the presence of his manly conduct, his ridiculous harlequin costume could be forgotten and his weakness for Russia overlooked. He resembled a proud stag which, although its flesh has been torn by the hounds, although it bears a mortal wound in its side, nevertheless holds its head high in its final hiding-place. But what was it about this strange

Turk that made me lose my sleep and disturbed my peace of mind?

Indignant chiefly with myself rather than with the Turk, I rose from my bed at first light and, dressing hurriedly and silently, I set off towards Kaynardja.

When I reached the spring I caught sight of Moskov Selim sweeping the front yard of his curious abode. I believe he saw me too standing by the spring in the half-light, but he was not surprised by my early appearance, nor did he display any particular haste this time to approach me. Dawn was already tingeing the horizon with crimson, and the breeze and the freshness of the morning lightened my head. I drank at the spring and felt invigorated. Then, making slowly towards the Turk's house I greeted him courteously.

"I hear you brew a good cup of tea in the Russian way," I said, "and I've come to try it. I'm very fond of tea when it's brewed in the Russian way."

Since others make fun of him for his pro-Russian sentiments, I thought to myself, let's begin from there and see where we get to.

The Turk straightened himself up with great dignity, returning my salutation with a slight wave of his hand, and fixed his large eyes, full of sorrow and perplexity, on my face.

"Alas!" he exclaimed. "What have the Russians done to make you dislike them? If only we did have some Russian tea to drink together! Here, come and sit down."

I peeped through the open door of the house.

"I see you have a samovar," I said, "but you seem to have run out of tea."

"Don't ask," he replied. "I never had any to run out. This samovar you see here, I had someone make it locally as best he could. The tea I brew with it isn't for you. I make it to comfort myself when I'm thinking. When I'm sitting alone I like to hear the water murmuring. Can you believe that?"

He went in and fetched a tin and showed me the contents. My nostrils were struck by a pleasing scent of thyme, mint, sage and other local medicinal flowers and herbs.

"Your tea is as curious as your samovar," I remarked.

The vessel, made of pieces of old tin untidily and inexpertly welded together, resembled a Russian samovar as much as Selim resembled a Russian soldier. And if Selim himself—I thought to myself—muscovizes no more than his tea does, then there is no danger of Turkey becoming russified.

"Sit down, please," repeated Selim. "I'll make you some nice coffee, and I've picked some fresh fruit, and there's milk for you too. The guide seemed to tell me you would come and chat with me. Sit here on this stool. Do you see that meadow down there, covered in mist? Now that's just like some places in Russia. Oh, blessed Russia!"

As he was speaking, Selim took down a basket full of ripe fruit that was hanging in the porch and placed it before me on a small stool, then went in to make the coffee and fetch the milk. The larks were vying with one another as they gradually ascended the fragrant air. The gushing waves of spring-water could be heard sweetly gurgling; in the branches of the beech tree a lone turtle-dove was lamenting its solitude. Joyous light from the east gilded the peaks of the hills towards the left and poured over the awakening brooks like a morning smile on the lips of a comely maiden. How could I have been deceived for so long the previous evening? What connection had this warm, balmy "painted meadow" and "purling stream" with the mute, dry and forbidding pictures of northern climes? True, at the furthest end of the spectacle before me a blanket of white mist was still spread over the marshy plains; but was this not the airy bed of Tithonus, from which, shortly before, rosy-fingered Dawn had risen? After a few moments the goddess' handmaidens, the breezes, would be snatching up its gossamer linens and laces on their wings, and the blanket would no longer impede the insatiable vision of the southern peoples. Were such spectacles to be seen in the sullen, sunless lands of Scythia?

"I hear you were a prisoner of war in Russia," I said to Selim as he returned with the coffee and milk. "May God never send you such a misfortune again."

"Don't blaspheme!" exclaimed the Turk in astonish-ment, almost dropping the coffee-ewers. "If you want me to be happy, wish me a prisoner in Russia!"

"I don't understand," I replied in surprise.

"It seems strange to you," he said, "because you don't know my story. It seems strange to others too, although I haven't told them outright. I've told you, though, so there it is. If you want me to be happy, wish me a pris-oner in Russia."

Selim sat down on the doorstep at the narrow en-trance to his little house and stretched out his legs in my direction with the characteristic indifference of his compatriots about such matters, so that I could see the soles of his feet protruding through his worn boots. The rest of his body took up more than two thirds of the height of the doorway. The dark room behind him acted as a background against which the Turk's strange, variegated dress and the pallor of his face stood out all the more starkly. It was then that I first noticed es-pecially the expression of his eyes from close at hand. Never had I seen eyes reflecting so profoundly and expressively that indefinable, mournful condition of the spirit which men are wont to call despondency. Re-alizing that as I sipped my coffee I was scrutinizing his expression, Selim lowered his eyes with a melancholy smile.

"You know, sir," he said, "you've done something extraordinary to me."

"May it be good," I replied in the Turkish manner.

"*Inshallah* (God willing), it is good," said he adding after a pause: "My heart beat faster when I saw you yesterday evening: I took you for a Russian. Don't ask me why. When I heard you deny you were a Russian, I thought how strange that such a good man isn't a Russian. You were in a hurry to leave, and I seemed to be in even more of a hurry. But after you left I felt very upset that I hadn't been able to stop you. I had a great desire to see you and talk to you—it's extraordinary! As soon as you went off on your horse, I ran off behind you like a bloodhound. But I was ashamed to call out to you, and you wouldn't have turned round anyway. Well, there we are! They told me at the village who you were. May God grant him prosperity, I said to myself, that's why he drew me along behind him. Well, if that's how it is, I told myself, he'll come back to Kaynardja, he's bound to. I was so sure you'd come back that when I saw you today I didn't think it at all strange."

"It was a correspondence of souls," I told him. "I too was unable to find peace of mind till I came back to see you."

"Really?" exclaimed Selim with childlike joy. "It's true, then, what they say, that two people can be complete strangers and yet their souls are like sisters!"

Lowering his voice a little, Selim devoutly declaimed the words of the Persian poet:

From the darkness of the earth
a hapless soul surveys the heavens,
and sees another soul up in the stars
happily smiling down upon it.
They both know they are kindred,
though separated by cruel Destiny.

"You're an educated man," continued Selim, resuming his former tone. "Tell me, in God's name, is it true that even stones would be lighter if they could find someone to tell their sorrow to?"

"Very true!" I replied, somewhat confounded by Selim's way of thinking. "Very true!"

"I imagine that's so," said Selim, "because I feel my heart becoming heavier and heavier with its sorrows, so that sometimes it seems to have turned to stone. Apart from the cold water that bubbles up out of the lifeless rock, I have no one to confide my troubles to. But even the water doesn't seem to want to listen sometimes, and it chatters away to itself more than I do, and by the time I turn round to look at it, it's gone by."

"If I may listen to your sorrows, Selim Aga," I told him, "I promise to sit right here without speaking. What secret troubles have you got in your heart?"

"I've nothing secret to relate to you," he said, "and no sorrow that can't be heard by others. But to other people Moskov Selim is more or less a madman. What can I tell them? How do you expect them to understand? That's why when I found out about you, sir, I breathed a great sigh. Such a man, I said to myself, must be as good as a Russian. If you tell your troubles to him, it's like telling the whole world. No one can accuse me of being a coward or a traitor—I'm determined to do what I told you earlier on. As soon as the Russians set foot in Turkey, I'll join their side; I'll become their ally; I'll go to their country and I won't come back. Am I right or am I wrong? You'll understand when you hear my story."

At this point I must confess that I wronged Selim, albeit only in my thoughts. Naturally, I could not begin to foresee the cause of his sorrow; but the way in which he broached the subject was so patently connected with his alleged pro-Russian obsession that I feared for a moment lest I had fallen into a trap laid by some clever monomaniac and had condemned myself to listen to matters of no great importance. But then I immediately bethought myself that the man who said these things was a Turk: he belonged, that is, to a nation whose particular characteristic is a profound contempt for whatever is inconsistent with their religion and traditions, a fanatical attachment especially to those superstitions which serve their national pride and egotism, and above all a stoically impassive acceptance of the vicissitudes of fate in both national and personal affairs. It would therefore be interesting, from many points of view, to hear the reasons for Selim's renunciation and rejection of his national character.

After having remained pensive for some time, as though he were trying to muster his strength, Selim bashfully lowered his eyes and began to relate his story in a weak, trembling voice that seemed to emerge from a rickety musical instrument.

"I was born into a family of rich beys. I had two brothers by the same mother. Since I was the youngest and we had no sister, our mother—bless her!—not only refused to let me leave the harem, but dressed me like a girl. The poor thing wanted to fool herself and console herself for not having a daughter. At the age of twelve I still had long hair, hennaed nails and rouged cheeks, and wore girl's clothes. My mother was all the more proud and fond of me—God forgive her!—because it was obvious I was the only one to take after her in every respect. While I was small, I suffered myself to be painted and dressed up like a doll, but as I grew older, so my disgust for women's caresses increased. This caused my poor mother great sorrow, since she saw I was impatient and couldn't wait to fly away from her arms. My father I saw very rarely: he was a proud, stern man and didn't talk much in the harem. He never used to take me on his lap and cuddle me: it was as if he were disgusted to see me with my long hair and girl's clothes. He was a very manly fellow: he loved horses and guns and made fun of women's business. Deep down, I worshipped him, and the more they insisted on keeping me in the harem the more fervently I desired to become an armed horseman like him!

"'I can see you don't love me,' my mother said to me one day as she stroked my hair. 'Poor child! Don't you realize your father has another wife now and doesn't want to know us any more? If you go with him too, I shall die, don't you see?'

"'But father has a beautiful charger,' I said, in my childish way, 'and he has golden pistols in his waist-band, that's why he has another wife.'

"'Very well, my lamb,' said my mother after ponder-ing sadly for some time. 'The *bayram* festival isn't far off. If you will love me as much as I love you, I'll buy you pistols then and anything else you want. Only give me your word that you won't become indifferent like your brothers.'

"As I said, I must have been about twelve and I reckon that, apart from the milk she had suckled me with, nothing could have made me more devoted to my mother than her promise to remove my girl's clothes and let me put pistols in my belt. As for love, I did feel immense love for her, and it was only for love of her that I had let myself be kept transmogrified and imprisoned for so long. But as soon as she gave me to understand that father was spurning her for the sake of another, I desired to show my love for her all the more. I never left her side, I never disobeyed her.

"'As long as you love me,' my mother—God forgive her!—often said, 'I'm not affected by other people's scorn. Look at your brothers: they've taken after their father; they've no heart in their breasts. You're the only one who's like me, God bless you!'

"The *bayram* soon came, and I suddenly found I was a little man with my tasselled fez, green double-breasted waistcoat and full pleated knee-breeches, gold-embroidered gaiters and, in fulfilment of mother's promise, two little pistols in my silk waistband. I was jumping for joy. First of all I ran to be embraced by my father. Now he wouldn't make fun of me, now he would like me. But my joy turned to sorrow when he saw me: his stern features darkened and he told me I didn't know how to walk like a boy!

"I'd thought to myself that if my father didn't love me as much as my brothers, it was the fault of my girl's clothes. So I expected he would look on me more favourably now that I was dressed like him, proudly riding my little horse and going to school. Not a bit of it. I was always the coward, the loathsome weakling. Whatever I did was wrong. My heart melted when I saw that my father simply refused to love me. Not only that, but he became angry when he saw that my eldest brother prevented our middle brother from bullying me.

"On the other hand, my mother, who got to know about everything, tried to keep me with her as long as possible in the harem on the pretext that she was teaching me my lessons. She was from a good family and had received some education. I wanted to be with her sometimes, because I saw she was unhappy and was greatly comforted when we were together and she could tell me how much pain her husband's second wife was causing her. My heart bled to hear her, but I could never bring myself to remonstrate with anyone and defend my mother against the wrong that was being done to her. For my only desire was to be loved by my father. So I always did what I knew would please him, and above all I tried to be the equal of my eldest brother, of whom the old man was very fond. He was the spitting image of our father, but he was gentle and kind-hearted. I often heard him singing my praises to father and trying to make him open his heart to me, but it was impossible. I became a fine lad of eighteen years old without ever having heard a kind word from his lips. Then one day they came to draw lots for the army, and the lot fell on my eldest brother.

"'I'm happy, very happy,' said my father when they brought him the news. 'The Serasker (Commander-in-Chief) is a relative of ours, and since it's your *kismet* to become a soldier, I want you to have a brilliant military career. I'll send a letter to the Serasker, and you'll do what I instruct you.'

"My brother changed countenance and stood with his arms folded, trembling like a leaf. My father, as I said, loved him more than the rest, but he was stern and unyielding: his will had to be obeyed.

"'It's nothing to be afraid of,' my father went on. 'If it's your fate to be killed by a bullet, then even if you hide at the bottom of the sea you'll still be killed by a bullet. I can hear the drum outside—the new recruits are gathering together to celebrate—come on, off with you and join your comrades.

"The sweat was pouring down my brother's face, and his eyes had dark rings around them. Father didn't turn to look at him. If I hadn't managed to put my arm under his to support him, he would have fallen in a faint. Father turned the other way, stood up from his cushion and without another word, not even a goodnight, went into the harem. Never had he entered the harem so early.

"It was towards evening; the drums were getting closer all the time; shouts rang out: 'Long live the Sultan!' Fiddles and lutes could be heard outside our door—they were coming to take him away. My brother hung round my neck, hid his face against my chest and with sobs that rent my heart and in a deep, deep voice of despair he cried:

"'I'm not going! I'll be killed in battle. I can't bear to go!'

"'Don't despair, master,' I said to him. 'There's still time before you go: father can still buy you out—if not, I'll go in your place, don't worry!

"The commotion had reached the top of the stairs: the green recruiting standard flew at the front, followed by the new recruits. Some were drunk on wine and opium; others were intoxicated without have drunk anything. But all of them looked joyful even if they weren't.

"'Come on, brother Hasan,' shouted the ensign, a short, fat, ill-mannered fellow. 'The Sultanate's giving us eight days' grace to enjoy ourselves as we please before joining the army. Come on! If you've had your eye on any beautiful Greek girl or you're holding a grudge against any of the infidels, come on: now's your chance to vent your frustration. Whatever any of you do now will be forgiven.'

"My poor brother! He resembled my father in his fierce, cruel looks, but no one could believe how mild and gentle he was in his heart. They were coming to take him as their leader in the beating, the killing, the thieving and the debauchery they were planning!

"The fiddles were playing downstairs; the servants had all gathered in the living-room; my brother was as white as a sheet. The standard-bearer took him aside and had a word with him. If it had been me, they would never have taken me with them. But my brother had no will-power. When he saw them with all their bluster, he seemed to give himself up to their designs. He hung his head and followed them. Never mind, I said to myself, let him go with them and enjoy himself. He'll take courage. Since father wants it so, he can't avoid joining the army. That night he didn't come home to sleep, and since my other brother managed to go off with them too, I, being the youngest, had to stay in the male quarters. The drums played all night, and twice I sent the servants out in case he had been made unpleasantly drunk. By midnight, nothing untoward seemed to have happened.

"First thing in the morning I went out to fetch him, because I'd heard my other brother come in alone and go to bed. I hadn't gone far before I saw the ensign with half a dozen new recruits behind him, hanging their heads and so drunk that they were lurching from wall to wall.

"'Where's my brother Hasan?' I asked him.

"'He's gone to the devil!' growled the other hoarsely. 'He left his comrades and went to the devil!'

"I was about to go on, when I saw the servant of a rich young man.

"'My brother was with your master last night,' I said to him. 'Do you know where he is now?'

"'He's still with him,' he replied with a knowing wink.

"'But where is he? At your house?'

"'God forbid!' said he. 'What do fledged birds like them want with a cage?'

"'I'm in no mood to listen to your nonsense,' I told him. 'Will you tell me what's become of my brother?'

"'I know right enough,' he replied impertinently. 'He's a deserter.'

"He hardly had time to say the word before I grabbed him so firmly by the throat that his eyes practically popped out of their sockets.

"'You cur!' I said. 'Take back that insult or I'll take away your life.'

"'Mercy! Mercy!' he moaned, half-throttled. 'Let me go and I won't tell. I haven't told anyone else.'

"'Come in here, you wretch,' said I, dragging him into the house.

"'It's not my fault,' he went on. 'I'm a servant and I just did what I was told. I got the horses ready and kept them waiting for them just outside the village. It was your other brother who brought the other necessaries. Didn't he tell you he helped him leave? It must have been two hours past midnight when we saw them off.'

"I put a florin in his hand.

"'Now watch out,' I said. 'If I hear you've been blabbing, you're a dead man!

"A couple of hours later I stood before the military council giving a verbal undertaking: 'Since my eldest brother's presence is essential to our family, I am willing to substitute for him by virtue of the right accorded me by law and custom.'

"Our family was of high standing, and my father could have bought my brother out if he'd wanted to. So the council put aside any nitpicking, and the clerk crossed out Hasan's name and wrote down mine. I swore the oath of allegiance to the Sultan and the flag and as I went out I wondered how I was going to report the matter to my father. The old man was pernickety and jealously proud and saw life itself as nothing in comparison with his reputation. In the eyes of the world I had saved our reputation: nobody had the right to call my brother a deserter, since it was I who had been re-cruited. But my father? My father had his own way of reckoning; how would he view what had happened?

"While I was going down the stairs with these things on my mind, a courier suddenly rushed into the court-yard of the headquarters, his horse bathed in sweat. It was an imperial decree: the recruits were to set off at once for Adrianople. I was called back and prevented from leaving, while the others were summoned to as-semble.

"I didn't yet know what it meant to be a soldier. I begged a minute's grace so I could nip over and say goodbye to my mother, but it was no good. Every face was stern, but as for the recruiting officer, God preserve you from such a look! The courier had come from the capital; people asked him the news, and soon everyone knew: the Empire was at war with Russia. The Crimean War had begun.

"With the roll-book in his hand, the major herded the recruits one by one into a stable; I was the first to be put there. He gave us such a look that anyone would think one of us had murdered his father. When I think of him now, I reckon I've never hated, and could never hate, anyone in the world more than that villain!

"'One moment! Just one moment! It's a matter of life and death. None of us knows whether he'll come back. Just one moment so I can kiss my mother's hand and receive her blessing!'

"'Impossible! Impossible!'

"When we were taken out into the yard in preparation for our departure, I made out my second brother amid the throng of people who had come to say goodbye to their loved ones. He didn't know what I'd done in the meantime, and he couldn't understand why I was lined up with the recruits.

"'Father gave me a letter and a purse to give to Hasan,' he said as he came up to me. 'He told me to say he sends him his blessing from the bottom of his heart, and that he should behave as a son of his should behave and should not bring shame on him. He wanted to come himself and say goodbye, but everything happened so suddenly that he was afraid his heart wouldn't be able to take it, and then people would say he was sorry his son was joining the army. Where's Hasan?'

"'You know very well the effendi my brother is somewhere he shouldn't be,' I replied, 'and with your help too. But, as you see, his place isn't empty. Now, if you don't want to get into trouble for doing that disgraceful favour, just listen to me. The police will be sent after the deserters with strict orders to arrest them. Since you know where they're hiding, run and save our brother. Nobody knows he's deserted because I made a deposition before he was asked for and, as you see, I was accepted as his substitute. Tell him to come back at once so word won't get out that he tried to escape and so our family honour won't be impugned.

As for father, tell him I kiss his hand and implore him to give me his blessing; tell him I begged Hasan to let me go in his place. I know how much father loves him and I didn't want him to be deprived of him in his old age.'

"I'd just managed to say all this, when suddenly the bugle sounded. We embraced with tears in our eyes— who knows whether we would see each other again?— the bugle sounded once more and the officers mounted their horses.

"'Take this ring,' I told him, 'and give it to my mother. If only she was a poor woman like the ones who are kissing their sons goodbye here in public, I would be able to see her once again before I leave and receive her blessing from her sacred lips. But she's a *hanum*, the daughter of a great bey: she can't leave the harem, and they didn't let me go there! Whenever she sees the diamond flashing against the gold, may she remember me and fancy she sees her son.'

The bugle sounded a third time. An imam slaughtered a sheep in front of the courtyard gate and the blood flowed in our path; then he raised his hands and prayed inwardly, giving us his blessing. Suddenly the deathly silence was broken by the fast, frenzied beating of the drum, the green standard was raised, and with all our heart we shouted: 'Long live the Sultan!'"

"So that's how I began my army career. Granted that right from the start I found everything quite different from what I'd expected; but no one can tell me I ever neglected my duty. Even the major who recruited us, a man who, if you pinched his noise poison would drip out of it, even he began to look on me favourably after a couple of days' march. I don't intend to describe every single thought that passed through my mind during the Crimean War. I gladly suffered all the pain and hardship and deprivation for the sake of my master the Sultan, and I shed my blood for him at Silistra as gladly as a mother parts with her milk to the baby she suckles. Just one thing stuck in my gullet—it was the first thing that saddened me, and I can't forget it. After we'd driven the Russians out of Silistra, I was found to have a serious wound that wouldn't heal as the others had. So two fellows carried me off to hospital in the fort. I must have lost a lot of blood, because I fainted and took some time to come round. When I began to regain consciousness and understand what was being said around me, I heard my name being mentioned over and over again by a couple of men who were nearest me. I paid closer attention and heard the story they were telling: I had suffered the wound so as to save our standard from enemy hands, after the ensign had fallen and the pale major had gone off, leaving us surrounded by the enemy. I reckon the wound healed the moment I heard the story rather than as a result of the ointments and bandages.

I wish I'd died then with that satisfaction! A doctor—I think he was a European—gave me to understand that a letter had been sent to our master the Sultan, who would put a medal on my wound as soon as I recovered and got out of bed, since I was such a brave soldier. But all that came to seem like a ruse to cure me as quickly as possible.

"When my wound was healed and I left the hospital, I saw the pale major, the deserter. He was hardly recognizable. The Serasker had promoted him by three ranks and pinned a huge medal on him for saving the standard from enemy hands! As soon as he recognized me, he beckoned me over.

"'A detachment's leaving for the Balkans today,' he said, 'to build fortifications. You'll go with them and dig and shift earth. Off with you, and don't let me see you round here again!'

"That was my reward and my medal! The European doctor explained it to me. The promotion and the medal had been sent by our master the Sultan for whoever had saved the standard from enemy hands. But that poisonous major was a relative of one of the Serasker's mistresses, so that not only was he not punished as a deserter, but he was decorated and promoted—all for the blood I shed while he was running away!

While I was ill I planned to write to my father to say I'd managed to achieve something in the fighting, and I was sure he would see to it that I was promoted, even now. He was a man who loved valour and prowess; the Serasker was still our relative, and what father had promised to my eldest brother when he enlisted, he could now do for me. But when I found out what it meant to have the Serasker as a relative, I thought to myself I could do without that! It was better that I should be the first to do my duty in the line of battle, knowing that nobody else would favour me but God and my *kismet*, than that I should be favoured in such a way. Who knows? Perhaps, amid the perils of battle, the devil might tempt me to remember that the Serasker was my relative, and I might betray my duty and desert! Then the Serasker might order the medal and the stripes to be given to me, his relative, while the brave lad who had saved the honour of the Empire and the standard of religion would not only go unrewarded, but suffer the ignominy, as I had done, of having his sword and rifle snatched from his hand and replaced by a bucket and spade! No, I knew what bitter disappointment this unjust treatment brought, and I didn't want anyone else to go through it. If I was to gain advancement, I wanted to do so through my own merits, not through influence and favour. These thoughts prevented me from writing to my father. Perhaps I should have written, though. Who knows, at least they would have learned I was alive. But from that time on my luck went so much against me that I never managed to send a letter home.

"I served the Sultan for seven whole years, but I didn't even have seven *paras* under my belt when I was given leave to return home. I'm not complaining, mind. All of us and our families, our lives and our fortunes are the property of our master the Sultan, and it's good fortune when they are expended in his service. But, out of pity and compassion for his people, the Sultan commanded that, just as every soldier is taken by the state from his front door, he should be sent back again and left at his front door. But what was I to do, abandoned barefoot and half-naked as I was, twelve days' journey from home?

"I can't tell you what I went through in order to get to our house. Let me just say I was thrown in prison three or four times by various nincompoops of officials because they were unable to read my pass and took me for a thief; and on three or four occasions they tried to execute me as a spy. So, having set off proudly and devotedly and with such high hopes for my military career, I finally returned humiliated, despised in my own country, not with the medal I had deserved to win in the heat of battle, but with wounds on my chest and a beggar's sack over my shoulder! Of course, my master the Sultan would never have wanted all this to happen, and I wasn't obliged to suffer it. And yet—if only those had been my only misfortunes!

"Nobody recognized me when I walked into our yard; but, believe me, I didn't recognize anyone either;

even the buildings had become unfamiliar. In my young day, wherever you looked everything you saw told you that the place was ruled by a strict master who loved order and beauty and tranquillity. But now everything was changed. The fountain in the yard had dried up; the iron rings on the doors had turned red with rust; and no one stood with his arms folded at the entrance, as before, ready to open the door to his master. I could hear the servants shouting shamelessly, swearing and laughing like maniacs; but none of them showed his face and looked to see who had come so as to inform the master. In dismay, with heavy heart and tearful eyes, I went upstairs to the living-room, where my father had been in the habit of sitting at that time of day. No one was there. Nevertheless, a great weight was lifted from my heart as I saw with relief that his weapons were hanging on the wall; his worry-beads, his pipe and all the personal belongings he used to have around him, were still there: father was all right! In my excitement I was not surprised that everything was quite covered in dust, and I didn't notice my old servant, who was rubbing his eyes to make sure whether it was really me or whether he was dreaming.

"'It's me, Sakirbaba,' I said. 'What are you goggling like that for?'

"'God is great, and great is His Prophet!' exclaimed the old man in astonishment, letting fall the stick he was leaning on. 'If you're my master Selim, strike me and take away my soul. God has lengthened my years so that I should live to see you in your mother's house with a beggar's sack over your shoulder!'

"'It's nothing,' I replied, 'nothing. I might have come in an even worse state than you see me in now. That was God's will. Can anyone who serves our master the Sultan fully and faithfully return home better than this?'

"'A thousand times no! I wish a thousand times, child of my soul, that you'd never done this service to the Sultanate, so my eyes wouldn't have seen what they've seen up to now!'

"'It was fated, Sakirbaba. Where's my brother Hasan? Where's my father? Go and inform my mother in the harem; have them send my clothes and heat the bath. And tell Hasan to join me in the bath-house if he wants. Find him and send him to me, do you hear?'

"'Oh Selim, Selim!' said the old man, his voice faltering in his throat. 'If only it were possible, even at the cost of my own life! You know nothing, then?'

"'What do you expect me to know? You're the first man I've seen in our house after so many years.'

"'Then it's a good thing God threw me in your path and you didn't meet any of your father's servants, or your father himself, for then your heart would have been broken by what's happened and what hasn't happened.'

"'So what has happened? Tell me quickly. I can see some misfortune has befallen us. What's happened?'

"'What hasn't happened,' said the old man, 'is what your father and the young *hanum* say has happened— that you're the cause of what's happened. As for what *has* happened… God is great, and great is His Prophet! Don't despair; sit there on the cushion. I'll tell you, as long as my poor heart can bear it. Don't stand there trembling—sit down! Nobody comes here, so nobody will hear. Ever since your father threw in his hand, none of the servants waits upon his masters. Because God's taken away his reason: your father's been bewitched, my son, and he's set up his abode in the harem. You know how he was! But now he's entrusted his beard to the arms of the *hanum* your stepmother.'

"'Sakirbaba!' I shouted. 'Why do you torment me so pitilessly? Why do you tear my heart to shreds, as though I were your worst enemy? Some great calamity has befallen me in this house—tell me at once what it is. Forget about love-affairs and bewitchments.'

"'Oh, child of my soul!' exclaimed the old man, bursting into tears. 'Your brother Hasan…'

"'Is my brother dead? Oh Lord, Lord!'

"'If only he'd simply died,' replied the old man, as I closed the floodgates of my own heart so as to hear him. 'If only he'd died as so many noble lords have ended their days, in the arms of their loved ones, when they've completed the time the Creator allotted them when he gave them souls to enter the world! If only he'd died as my own brave boy died, on the soil of Crimea, with his

— 57 —

sword in his hand, for our religion and our Caliph, to be a consolation to us as he enjoys the grace and beauty of Paradise amid its flowers and blossoms! Oh, master of my soul—Hasan your brother was killed, unjustly killed!'"

As he related this scene, Selim's voice faltered and his tears flowed copiously.

"I don't have to tell you," he resumed after a long pause, "what a sudden and fearful blow that was to my heart. I confess that up to that point I was afraid I might hear that my mother was suffering or had suffered some calamity. When I heard about my brother's death I inwardly thanked God for pitying me at least as much as to spare my mother. I told you how I parted from her, how much I loved her and how much her life depended on my love. But when I heard my brother had been killed and my father believed me to be responsible, I was rooted to the spot by grief and astonishment.

"The servant was a kind old soul and loved us with all his heart. He used to take us out when we were young, he used to take us to school and fetch us home again. Our mother used him as her confidant whenever she wanted to find out how father was treating us, or to give us a message or send us anything, once we had grown up and weren't allowed into the harem. For this reason he was more devoted to us and our mother than to my father and his second wife. When at last he managed to hold back his tears, I learned what had happened in our home since I had left. I'll explain myself briefly.

"As soon as the recruits had left in hot haste, my father presented himself to the court and denounced my brother Hasan as a deserter. The judge and the mufti assured him that Hasan couldn't have deserted since I, his brother, had given an undertaking and replaced him according to law and custom.

"'I have witnesses,' insisted my father, 'that my son, who's liable for military service, escaped into the hills at night with a comrade of his and hasn't yet returned. No one has a legal right to substitute for a deserter, and one who's been drawn by lot too. As soon as my son left he became a deserter, and since I will not tolerate such a disgrace in my family, I demand that he be arrested, like any other deserter, and suffer double the punishment by being forced to carry out his duties in chains. The enemy has set foot on the soil of our master the Sultan, and a fine lad, who's been raised amid the bounty granted us by our master in his compassion, and who's grown up with my example, goes off and deserts? If you don't send the mounted police after him and arrest him, I'll denounce your villainy to the Serasker himself. As for his brother, he might replace some young girl in her domestic duties, but not Hasan in war! Whatever he's done is his own responsibility. I will tolerate nothing and recognize nothing. He's deceived the law and concealed the deserter: it's your duty to punish him.'

"The fiercest and most bloodthirsty policemen were sent into the hills, where they supposed Hasan and his companion were hiding. They didn't have to look far; but the lads were armed and put up a fight. My brother's companion had powerful connections and was certain that, whatever he did, he had nothing to fear; he simply had to avoid being caught while the Empire had need of soldiers. So they put up a fight from the high rocks where they were hiding, and they wounded one of the policemen. Then the others threw themselves at them like dogs, besieged the lads behind a rock and, when their bullets ran out, they charged with their swords. The other lad managed to escape unobserved through a gap in the rocks, while my brother was found dead, slumped over his bastion, drenched in blood. The bullet had pierced his forehead just as he was taking aim.

"When the news reached my father, he showed no sign of grief.

"'God has triumphed,' he said. Let it be an example to others. What is written is written. It was written that he should die by the bullet. He didn't go to the wars, and his life was wasted. Go and dig his grave!'

"'But as soon as Hasan was buried and his absence in the house became perceptible, your father began to change,' the old servant told me. 'This man who had once been so strict within his own halls, who took such care over his estates and who never touched a drop of drink—he's now become the most pitiful character. He neglects his estates and has no care for the house, but just sits like a dummy in the harem from morning till night with the raki bottle in front of him.

"'Your second brother got married and left five years ago. Your stepmother managed to persuade him to transfer all his property to her name. You know, she has no children and ever since the misfortune happened with your eldest brother she's never stopped assuring your father that you inveigled him into taking to the hills so as to wound his self-esteem—to show him that the son he loved didn't take after him, to become an obstacle to his future prosperity—that sort of thing and worse. And he believes it, because he hears nothing else. If you could see him in the harem now, an old man with a snow-white beard, sitting and ogling the naked slave-girls she gets to dance in front of him, how he lets them kiss him and pet him and sing the songs she's taught them, just so she can make him so befuddled with drink and debauchery that he'll soon die and leave her to marry someone her own age!'

"'Oh, my poor mother!' I exclaimed. 'I can imagine what sorrow all this causes my poor, good mother!'

"'You need have no worries on that score,' replied the old man pensively. 'She has no more sorrows to bear, thank God... When you went off like that without her seeing you and talking to you, she called me and said, "Sakirbaba," she said, "I shan't be able to bear this grief!" Then the calamity happened with her other son. You see, she was a good, saintly woman, and what she said came true. Every day that passed seemed to gnaw away some of her health and life and brought her closer to the grave… Every so often she would call me to ask me about the war and what news there was of you. You'd gone off and cut your ties with your family, and no word came from you till now. So I used to talk to her and comfort her.

"'She wore a diamond ring on her finger, and it seemed to her to be getting duller all the time. "It's the tears in your eyes, Hanum Effendi, that prevent you seeing how it sparkles," I used to tell her. But she wouldn't believe me.

"""This dullness bodes badly," she said. "My son's life is in danger. He's wounded, he's dying!" The more the life ebbed from her eyes, the duller the ring appeared to her.

"'One day—I remember it as if it were yesterday—she sent for me again to find out what news had come from the young master, her son.

"""Someone who's just come down from the Danube," I told her to comfort her, "has brought the news that the Muscovites have been defeated and our master Selim's received a medal and a high rank from the Sultan."

"""What am I to do with them?" she said, her sweet face radiant like a sorrowful angel's. "My eyes have grown dim from looking into the street to see if my son's coming. I can't see whether the ring he left me is still shining!"

"'Then she took it off her white finger and gave it to the Circassian who sat by her bedside.

"''There, Meleyka," she said. "I bought you as a slave; you've loved me and cared for me as if I were your own mother. Before God and these witnesses I grant you your freedom. I haven't had the good fortune to see the light of my eyes, the love of my heart… Hide the ring I'm giving you as safely as you can! If you're luckier than I am and my son, my master, returns, I leave you in my place to love him and care for him. He's faring badly in distant lands and I don't want him to find himself alone in the world when he comes home!"

"'These words seemed to be spoken by some heavenly spirit hidden in her breast. She spoke so sweetly, so calmly, with a celestial smile on her face, that none of us dared say a word. Then she fell asleep and I went about my business. After a while we heard the women weeping from the male quarters:

"''Our great *hanum* has delivered up her spirit to God!'"

"My tears poured down my cheeks all the time my old servant was talking, and I went on weeping for a long time after he had finished. I wept for the dead and I wept for myself, who had now come to live, hated and alone, in the situation that the old man had described.

"I sent him to tell Meleyka the Circassian secretly that I'd arrived, to ask for whatever clothes of mine could still be found, and to bring them to me at the public baths.

"When I returned home again it was late in the evening. Everyone had found out that I'd come—everyone, that is, except my father. His wife mustn't have let anyone tell him, I presumed, so next day I sent Sakirbaba to inform him.

"'Light to your eyes, Bey Effendi!' he said. 'Your son's come back from abroad, your soldier!'

"'I have no son who's a soldier,' he retorted. 'My son who was to have been a soldier will never return from where he's gone. Don't let me set eyes on the one who's just arrived!'

"Through all the hardships I had suffered in the service and through all the trials I had undergone on my travels, I always had, tucked away, the consolation that I would at last win my father's love. My body was covered in wounds, large and small; he would only have to see them, I said to myself, in order to realize that I had inherited his courage and valour and that I was a brave warrior. I resembled him in character even though I didn't take after him in looks. He was bound to take me into his arms at last and kiss me. Such—and more— were the thoughts I used to think to myself. I even hid my identity when I arrived in our district so as not to offend his self-esteem with the terrible state I was in.

"It would have been better if a bullet had pierced my heart while I was seeking to gain his love in the tumult of battle, than that I should come and find so much hatred in him after I had been deserted by all those who loved me.

"I stayed in the house by myself for two days. Then on the third day I was led off to court.

"'Some years ago,' said the judge, 'you were tried and condemned for hiding a deserter and deceiving the Sultan. The deserter was your brother and the plaintiff your own father. He's renewed his case against you and you'll go to prison for one year.'

"In any other circumstances I would have been clever enough to get out of such a sentence by arguing my way around the judge. But I accepted the sentence in order that my father's will should be done. In any case, our house was worse than a prison for me in the state I had found it. God bless Sakirbaba—he let me want for nothing. Besides, I didn't have to feel any shame or suffer any disrespect, since everyone knew that I was the victim of my father's spite, and they pitied me and looked after me as if I were their master. I wouldn't of course have received such treatment in my father's house.

"So the year went by, and as it neared its end I became more and more downcast. My second brother sold the estates he'd received from his wife and moved to Anatolia. I would be condemned to living at home.

I had no hope of reaching an understanding with my father in his condition. Then we suddenly learned that revolution had broken out in Herzegovina. I lost no time, but immediately put on a set of silver armour, mounted a stallion, and off I rode.

"Sakirbaba had often found occasion to sing the praises of Meleyka's beauty and kindness. It was she who cooked the food he brought me in prison, and she arranged for anything I needed from home to be sent to me, just as if my own mother were still alive. A secret voice told my heart that since my mother had given the ring to this girl she would be my *kismet*. But you can't imagine what came over me when I heard about the war: I was determined to go and seek my *kismet* once more amid the smoke and fire of battle. I wasn't fated to enjoy home life and family happiness. So off I went.

"God granted that the commander who took me into his battalion happened to be a brave man, and per-haps for that reason a fair-dealer. When I returned home two years later, I bore a few extra wounds, but I had a slightly higher rank and a medal for bravery.

"This time I was able to see my father in the male quarters. My father! If I wasn't his own son I wouldn't have recognized him! What had become of his proud forehead, his flashing eyes and his broad chest? It was as if he'd been ill in bed all those years since I had last seen him; his face had grown pale, his brow was furrowed, his body had become bent, and his arms and legs trembled like a leaf. That's the state his new wife had brought him to!

"When I went in and kissed his hand, he raised his sunken eyes and gazed at me searchingly, then two teardrops trickled down his pale cheeks.

"'You take after your mother!' he said. 'She was a good woman, but… she's dead. As for that vixen, when I'd written all my fortune over to her, she threw me out of the harem!'

"'What's that, Effendi?' said I. 'In our family it's unheard of for a woman to throw her master out of his own house!'

"'It's a mystery to me too,' he replied with childlike puzzlement. 'But I can't help loving the hussy all the same! Pour some raki and we'll drink to her health!'

"Such was the degree to which his manly character had been ruined by drink, and such was the state in which I renewed my acquaintance with my father!"

Selim went on to recount how his father's physical and moral decrepitude had brought about a similar frailty in the family's financial affairs. The herds had gradually been sold off, the stables and cowsheds were empty, and the best of their estates had fallen into the hands of creditors and money-lenders, to whose coffers the old landowner had resorted whenever his young wife needed to satisfy some new whim. One piece of land, which was part of his mother's dowry, still remained unencumbered; Selim personally undertook to cultivate it, as his father had done formerly, and in a short time he had succeeded in improving it to such an extent that even the feeble-minded old man had to admire it.

"You take after my good wife!" he used to say occasionally. "You are the child of my soul!"

Then, forgetting the old man's cruel and unjust behaviour towards him, Selim would fling himself round his neck, attempting in such an embrace to slake the thirst for paternal affection that had dogged him for so long. But when the kisses and embraces had ceased, Selim experienced the kind of disappointment felt by a thirsty wayfarer who, having strayed far from his route with the sole wish of drinking his fill from a life-giving spring that he knows well, suddenly finds its waters have dried up. The father he embraced was no longer the one he had once admired, the one from whom a single glance of affection would have made him wild with joy. The father he kissed was a drunken old imbecile, rendered feeble through such an extended abuse of alcoholic liquor that he no longer had a clear conception of anything except whether he was drinking or not. His intellect had been devastated by his debauchery, his heart had been withered by over-indulgence, and there was no paternal affection or dignity left in him.

For this reason Selim expedited his union with Meleyka, his mother's emancipated Circassian slave.

"I could have married into a rich family," he said, "and made good what my father had squandered. But my mother was a saintly woman—may the earth where she lies become musk and amber!—and since she had given my ring to Meleyka, that meant she was my *kismet*."

His mother's choice was indeed worthy of respect, for Meleyka was endowed with all manner of virtues. She cared for her feeble father-in-law with filial self-denial and helped Selim partake in as much connubial bliss as was possible in the circumstances. By the time the last revolt in Herzegovina broke out in 1875, Selim was a wealthy landowner with three beautiful, lively children.

"If I hadn't been married," said Selim, "I wouldn't have hesitated for a moment, so indignant was I to learn that all our efforts and all the blood we had shed in 1862 had been for nothing. But the children were small and father was ill, and I was champing at the bit to think there was a war going on against the Sultan.

"Before long Serbia was up in arms, and Bulgaria as well. The Empire was calling up reservists. I remember my turn hadn't come round yet; but when I heard Russia was making preparations too, I didn't wait my turn; I didn't think twice about it or consult anyone. You know we think of the Russians as the arch-enemy of our nation. Fire and water may make friends with each other one day; but Muscovy and Islam—never! You see the Tartars and the Circassians who've left their homes and their belongings to come to the Empire of the Sultan, naked and barefoot, rather than live with the Russians?

"So I left my children, my wife and my fortune and signed up with the reservists. Fortune, wife and children are all the Sultan's property, and when we were fighting the Muscovites, even if I had nine lives I would have laid them all down in battle to enable our master to win! We fought Russia, as I told you, at the time of Crimea, and we beat them hollow at Silistra. That enmity and hatred I'd felt against Russia was redoubled when I heard they were coming to invade our territory again. They were seeking to wipe us off the face of the earth, and I would gladly have eaten them alive if I could! So off I went to the wars.

"First we were led against Serbia, and it was clear that Russia wanted our downfall there too. I don't know what the newspapers said about the Turks at that time, but I fought at Aleksinac that autumn, and I can assure you we regained control of the whole country and made it ours again. But it was all to no avail! A piece of paper from the Tsar was all it took to make the Serasker order us to leave Serbia! My God give them their just deserts! It was like ordering someone to leave a house he'd built with his own life's blood and his own bones.

"So we withdrew, for the sake of peace and concord, they said! Ha! That shows you the great wisdom of the Sultan's Serasker and the other hangers-on that make up our state! As you know, the Muscovites achieved their aim: before we had time to heal the wounds we'd received in Serbia, the Russians had crossed the Danube! Whereupon, instead of returning home to get cured, I forgot my fever and my tremors and about-turned. The Russians have set foot on the Sultan's soil, I said to myself; how can Selim go off home now? I had an unhealed bullet-wound in my left arm, and I still had the arm in a sling. But as soon as I met some troops, I untied the sling, gritted my teeth so as not to feel the pain, and presented myself to their commander. At that time they would have made soldiers out of tombstones if they could! I was a sergeant, so he accepted me without much of an examination and off we went. After all the fighting and killing in the Balkans, I seem to have been fated to see myself captured and imprisoned at Plevna.

"Ah, Plevna, Plevna!" sighed Selim, continuing his story ruefully. "It was Plevna that brought me to my senses. As God's my witness, when I reached Plevna I felt as if I were drunk and crazy. Whenever we found the Russians hiding anywhere this side of the Balkans, we thrashed them. It was the first time since Crimea that I'd seen them in front of me, and each of them looked to me to be seven times more evil than the devil! 'The arch-enemy of our nation, damn him!' I used to say whenever I found one of them helplessly wounded, and I would finish him off with ferocious glee.

"When I entered Plevna I was a captain. Plevna was renowned for its first heroic resistance; so imagine with what joy and hope I led my men, how eagerly I held my sword, and with what acclaim we saluted Osman Pasha, the old hero of Plevna. We had come as reinforcements for his troops—3,000 men—and, wherever we might go, the Russians wouldn't be able to stop us.

"'Here at last I'll be able to vent my hatred,' I told myself. 'Here I'll take pitiless revenge on our savage, ruthless foes, the Russians!'

"When the moment came to open fire on them that September, my enthusiasm knew no bounds. I felt that every bullet we fired at them took strength from my own heart to strike as deeply and destroy as unsparingly as possible. Whenever we fought with bayonets and swords, I was always among the first. But what's written by fate can't be altered.

"I received a bullet wound in my right lung which removed me from my post and put me in hospital. It was a very severe wound. Winter came and I still couldn't move; I was spitting blood.

"I wasn't aware of anything important happening all that time; but suddenly one evening I realized the doctors, the hospital staff and the walking wounded had all gradually begun to slip out. There was a lot of whispering and groaning and cursing, then dead silence; so I stood up. It was dark and I couldn't make anything out clearly, but in the distance I could hear troops marching towards the river. That wasn't a good sign! The Russians had surrounded us inside our fortifications and there were no more provisions left in Plevna.

"Obviously Ghazi Osman Pasha had been forced to withdraw. I looked around and found the streets deserted. There was nobody with me: those who had stayed behind must have been worse off than me. I picked up my greatcoat and, dressed as I was, I ran out into the darkness. On my way I met other wounded men limping along on crutches. They were hurrying along as fast as they could, groaning and weeping and cursing. I was furious. I pulled myself together and managed to find a battalion marching along in silence, and another one coming down towards me from the side.

"'Go back quickly!' shouted an officer on horseback, who had recognized me as one of the wounded. 'You'll get killed round here! Go back!'

"'I'm Captain Selim! I said. 'How can I go back? As long as I could hold a rifle and draw a sword, the order was always "advance!", but now I'm wounded you're ordering me to retreat. Either take me with you or kill me on the spot! Nobody's stayed behind. Are you abandoning me to the enemy?' I stood in front of him and grabbed the bridle of his horse.

"'If you revere the Prophet Mohammed,' I told him, 'draw your sword and cut off my head! I've been a soldier of the Sultan for twenty-five years—how can you forsake me and let me be taken alive by the enemy?'

"I hadn't had time to finish before the horse, feeling the prick of the spurs in its flanks, reared over me and knocked me flat on my back. I felt several soldiers walk over my wounded chest, then I fainted…

"When I came to, it was dawn. I felt as if I were dreaming. My knee was hurting badly and I couldn't move it. Then I remembered the horse, my fall, and the feet trampling over my chest. May God punish the merciless villains! Next I recalled everything I had achieved in the wars over so many years; I thought how much better it would have been if I'd been killed by a shot in the firing-line, and I was seized by inexpressible horror. What new sufferings lay in store for me at the hands of the enemy?

"Then I heard cannon-fire from down beyond the river: the battle had begun. Allah! Allah!—but the prayer for my brothers refused to come to my lips! I couldn't say, 'God help them!'—so great was my resentment against them for having abandoned me into the hands of the enemy. I was unable to tell what was going on down there, but I realized Plevna was no longer ours. My sorrow and despair, the state of my health and the intense cold all combined to make me feel numb and confused, and I didn't know what I was doing. I was completely unarmed; God—no, not God, but my fellow Muslims—had yielded me up as a sacrificial victim to the enemy. Now each of them would be quite justified in avenging himself on me according to my thoughts and deeds. Let them come! Let them tear me to pieces and throw me to the dogs! And so, exhausted as I was, I dragged myself along and fell to the ground near a rock, wrapped in my greatcoat.

"When I came to myself, I found that I was in a field hospital, and I learned that I was a prisoner of the Russians along with all those in Plevna—40,000 soldiers, including Osman Pasha himself and many other pashas too.

"It's not easy for me," resumed Selim after a brief pause, "to describe what changes occurred in my feelings from then on; but perhaps it will be easy for you to guess when you've heard the rest of my story."

Selim attempted to picture for me the surprise he felt when he saw the humanitarian compassion with which the Russian doctor, and the Sisters of Mercy who assisted him, healed his wounds in a few days, dressing him and feeding him even better than the pashas in Plevna had fared. Blinded by fanaticism against the Russians, he had imagined them to be cruel, bloodthirsty and ready to tear his raw flesh apart like savage beasts. And yet these were Russians that he saw before him, and he found them polite and solicitous as they tried in various ways to console the prisoners for their fate, to give them courage for the future and to assure them that, even as prisoners, they excited the admiration of the Russians and of the whole world for the courage and valour with which they had fought. Selim especially, by virtue of the large number of wounds which he had received over the years and whose scars the doctor examined carefully, seemed to them to be a man of particular worth. They gave him to understand that if the Tsar had only such soldiers as Selim, he would be Sultan of the whole world. This flattered the soldier's self-esteem, since he had rarely heard even a "bravo" for feats of valour which among other nations are royally rewarded. After a while Selim was sent to Russia along with the rest of the prisoners.

For reasons of political expediency the Russians lavished almost unbelievable attentions on the Turks captured in that war. Tears came to Selim's eyes as he related the warm, friendly reception he was given wherever he went. The Russian peasants greeted their captured enemies by addressing them as *bratushka* (brother)!

Wherever the train stopped, they were offered tea and other warming drinks; whenever they left their carriages, the local people embraced and kissed them. All this brought about a veritable revolution in the feelings of Selim, whose heart was essentially kind and sensitive. So these were the implacable foes of his nation, who wanted to wipe the Turks off the face of the earth? What a mistaken idea he had had about Russia!

"I'd been crazy up to then," Selim added. "That's why I said that Plevna brought me to my senses."

At Plevna Selim had observed the deprivations and ill-treatment suffered by the few Russian prisoners, and had therefore expected to suffer equally, if not worse, in Russia. Instead of this, throughout his imprisonment Selim ate copiously, dressed in warm, clean clothes, heard tender and consoling words such as he had never heard at home; and, most important of all, he and his fellow prisoners were left free and unhindered to perform their religious observances in specially constructed buildings. Such a thing would never have been permitted by the enemies of Islam! Thus it is not strange that Selim should have altered his views about the possibility of Muslims and Russians living side by side, and described as foolish those who struggled against the invasion of European Turkey by the Russians.

"God's world is large," he said, "and if the poor Tsar has difficulty in accommodating his subjects, let them come to our country—they're such good people. What would it cost the Sultan? He enjoys himself in Constantinople, so why can't he enjoy himself in Baghdad or Damascus? Can't we live with our brothers the Russians? *Bratushka! Bratushka!*"

Thus did the political good sense of the Russians seek to bridge the vast chasm separating them eternally from the Turks. What they had not achieved with the lion-skin they were now bringing about surreptitiously with the fox-skin. About 100,000 Turkish soldiers, led away into captivity, were flattered into believing that they were not the Russians' prisoners but their guests; and consequently in future they owed the Russians the same polite treatment that the religion of Mohammed commands its faithful to afford to all those under whose rooves they have tasted bread and salt as guests.

As for Selim, at the other end of the bridge spanning that chasm, the burning flame of love, like a beacon, signalled to him from afar to hasten his return to Russian arms.

"To experience beauty is a supreme good," said Selim, broaching the subject with some embarrassment. "I met an old officer who had come to Adrianople in 1829; he remembered a little Turkish and invited me home for tea. He had a widowed daughter, who looked after him—may God preserve her for her father!—she was a real angel! Her husband, who was a proper rake, had courted her for years before he succeeded in gaining her hand. But he wasn't married to her for long. After squandering all her fortune at cards in five or six weeks, he grabbed a pistol and blew his brains out. A proper rake! So the poor woman had been a widow for six years. The old man loved cards too, and he used to play with Pavloshka to pass the time, but once we'd become acquainted he wouldn't let me alone. He used to tell me all about the wars he had fought in, and it pleased him a lot to hear me praise the Russians.

"The fair Pavloshka only understood as much as her father explained to her, and used to shake her head

and wag her finger, indicating that the Russians aren't
good because they get drunk and go in for gambling
—whereas Selim, who doesn't drink and gamble—
harashó, harashó! She used to say this with such a sweet
voice and such looks—I can't tell you! My wife, Meleyka, was beautiful and good, but—how can I explain
it? In our homes the best women behave like sheep. I
had lived for years with Meleyka and we had three children. But—would you believe it?—she never looked
into my eyes as Pavloshka did. When I looked at her,
Pavloshka didn't lower her eyes with humility like a
servant who bows his head to be commanded or chided
by his master. No, I felt as though a sweet fire was en-
tering my heart, lighting it up, warming it, thawing it
out, giving it wings and making it fly up to heaven with
happiness and joy—but making it feel it would rather
fly into Pavloshka's arms! And her voice! Her singing!
Granted, I didn't understand their language, but that
was just why her singing touched my heart-strings so
powerfully. After all, nobody can understand a nightin-
gale's language, and yet whoever hears it feels it's
singing about pains and torments and love. God preserve her for her father! For nights on end I lay awake
in bed thinking and crying like a baby because God
hadn't made my Meleyka like that, for all her beauty
and goodness.

"But Meleyka had the ring my mother had given her;
I couldn't possibly leave her, but my heart was sorely

wounded. And when the war ended and the time came for us to be sent back home, that was when I realized I couldn't leave Russia without leaving part of my soul behind!

"And so, after all my happiness as a prisoner of war," Selim continued agitatedly, "after all the care and hospitality I had received at the hands of the enemy, just listen to the welcome we got from our own people; listen to the treatment that the Empire we had served almost to the death handed out to its warriors."

Selim described his subsequent adventures in the gloomiest of colours.

The prisoners were conveyed by rail to the nearest ports with the utmost care and attention. Wherever they went, crowds of people bade them farewell, always addressing them by the sweet name of "brother", and up to the very last moment showed as much affection as possible towards the departing Turks.

Each of the prisoners without exception bore with him some memento given him by his acquaintances. Selim was accompanied by Pavloshka and her father to the sea, where they embraced and parted amid floods of tears. But, for all of them, the comfortable life ended there at the quayside; there every prisoner was obliged to leave behind anything Russian he had about him and put on the filthy rags he had worn for so long on the field of battle; and thus, most of them half-naked and barefoot, they boarded the steamers in their hundreds and thousands, crammed mercilessly even into the bowels of the ships together with the ballast. When they reached the capital of the Empire, they cursed the day that they had been invited to return to their sweet homeland!

The return of the prisoners took place in mid-winter. Constantinople was still inundated with the refugees from Bulgaria who had flooded every public building as well as most of the larger private houses. Even the mosques became the living-quarters of women and children, who crammed them full; and many of these wild creatures, rendered yet wilder by despair, could be seen camping in the streets.

Where were the prisoners to be housed on their return? No provision had been made for them. They were disembarked on the Galata Bridge and on the shores of the Bosporus, starving, shivering and in a dire state from the frightful voyage. The officers accompanying them went off to military headquarters as soon as they landed, and the warriors of Plevna, numbering more than 40,000, together with a similar number of other prisoners, found themselves, after a life of luxury in an enemy land, suddenly facing death from starvation and exposure in full view of the magnificent institutions on whose behalf they had so often exposed themselves to danger.

"When I consider," said Selim, "that, after so many battles and so many heroic deeds, the Sultan's soldiers were reduced to taking alms from the Jews, while the delicate effendis walked past with their silk umbrellas and their gloves, pretending not to notice us, my heart seethes with anger! God had removed pity from Islam!"

Before long, however, the patience of these unfortunate creatures was exhausted, the courtyard of the military headquarters was besieged, and thousands of voices demanded the back pay owed to the soldiers for so many years, the pay they had earned through hardship and the shedding of their own blood, so that each one might return to his own home. But—according to Selim—the grandees had squandered so much of the nation's wealth that there was nothing left with which to pay the soldiers. Since these latter began to stir up desperate disturbances in the streets, the authorities were forced to round them up into the precincts of the great mosques and provide them with paltry rations, pacifying them with the promise that they would soon receive what was owing to them. Typhoid had already decimated the throngs of refugees, and the unfortunate soldiers, concentrated into the same precincts as the sick, began dying by the hundred. Fearing the justifiable indignation of these men, the police took the precaution of confiscating every weapon they might be carrying. Thus, while Selim was lying in the cold mire in a makeshift tent, in a high fever and without anyone to help him, he heard a young policeman demanding to be handed the Russian cutlass which he happened to be holding. Selim had managed to bring this cutlass, despite all adversities, to Constantinople: it was a valuable keepsake from his beloved Pavloshka.

"Imagine," said Selim, "how I felt at the audacity of that whipper-snapper. As if all my frightful tremors and the generally pitiful state of my health weren't enough, he had to come and plunge a knife into my heart. I refused to hand over the weapon; and when he tried to wrench it away from me, I leapt up, grabbed him round the neck and sent him rolling in the mud.

"'You cur!' I said. 'Even the Muscovites weren't able to snatch a weapon from the hands of Captain Selim!'"

The result of Selim's precipitate action was that in the evening he was led in a sorry state to the police, where he was mercilessly beaten and not only deprived of the cutlass but stripped of the stripes on his greatcoat which denoted his rank.

"Why are you wearing these in the streets and begging?" they demanded sternly. "You want to shame the state? You're no longer a soldier, let alone an officer. Get out of here!"

"Now I ask you," continued Selim after having given me a detailed account of these events, "who's to blame in this world—the murderer or his victim? That fearful idea occurred to me after they'd untied my hands, and it wouldn't have been at all difficult to slaughter them all on their velvet-covered chairs. But I'd lived a just and honest life till then, and I didn't want my name to be sullied. 'You've got a wife and children at home, Selim,' I said to myself. 'If you've nothing else to give them, at least preserve your good name.' So God gave me patience, and I dragged my sick carcass around the streets of Constantinople for a couple more months till the snows melted and the roads opened and I was able to crawl slowly back home.

"Back home!" repeated Selim after a brief pause, smiling his bitter, woeful smile. "That's what I thought, poor fool—that I was coming back home to my wife and children to be looked after, to recuperate, to start a life of work again, since I wasn't fated to die after all these torments. My home! Where was my little home? Where were my wife and children?

"While we were protecting the Sultan's throne and the very existence of the Empire beyond the Balkans, the effendis who stayed behind to govern the district and defend it got together with the Circassians and the refugees who were fleeing from Bulgaria and fell on Christian villages and houses, killing and pillaging. They felt brave enough then! But when Plevna fell and the Muscovites poured down this side of the Balkans, those people felt retribution was coming to them and they would get their just deserts for the evil crimes they'd committed; so they abandoned their houses and rushed headlong down to Constantinople to save their skins. My father was no longer alive: raki had been the death of him, God forgive him! His wife had already sold all our estates when she became the sole mistress of the house, and she took her money and went off and got married in Constantinople. My share of the property—60,000 piastres—was placed in trust by the mufti to be left to my children in case I never returned. But it never rains but it pours, and when my poor wife heard the Muscovites were coming—I'd left her helpless in order to help the state!—she joined the other families and fled to Constantinople.

"You can easily imagine what happened next. When the Christians who had fled into the hills learned that the Turks had left, they came back and set fire to our houses in revenge. Half the Turks, who left in the middle of winter, perished before they reached Constantinople, and of those that arrived, there were many who never lived to return. Famine, cold and pestilence robbed me of my wife and children.

"A wife and three children," shouted Selim, wiping away his tears, "perished before their appointed hour of death had come, in sight of the very throne of that Sultan that I had defended so many times in my life. They were mine, and the last things left to me in the world!"

The poor wretch bowed his head and a look of woeful dejection darkened the pallor of his kind features. Then, leaping up from his seat with a frown, he exclaimed:

"Now I defy anyone who's been created by God with heart and breast to come and condemn Selim for his convictions! God has taken away his pity from this country because of the evildoings of the effendis and the agas, and he's made our land the *kismet* of Russia because of her benevolence and good sense. Don't you see it yourself? Where are Silistra and Herzegovina now? Where are Serbia and Bulgaria? Wherever we were once victorious we've now been defeated! That's why I don't want to know any more about it. It's my *kismet* and my right to live the few more years God has granted me just as I please. I haven't concealed from anyone how I want to live, as you can see for yourself. But people don't want to find out my reasons, that's why they call me stupid, and they may even call me a wicked turncoat when they hear Selim's joined the Muscovites."

"No one will dare call you that, I assure you," I said. "Now that I've heard your story, no one will say that. You're a noble man, Selim Aga, and you've been sorely wronged."

"God bless you and preserve you in joy and happiness!" said the poor man from the bottom of his heart, clasping my hand. "My heart's been relieved of a burden today—may God reward you for it. I've never known such pleasure in the midst of sorrow! Just one thing I beg of you: when you read in the papers that the Russians are coming again, let me know as quickly as you can. I'll sprout wings, I assure you, so as to go and join them."

"I'm going to the capital very shortly and I hope to return from there in a month, or two at the most," I told him. "Then I'll come especially to see you and tell you what we are to expect this winter. What is certain is that things are simmering again in Bulgaria: the Russians don't approve of Prince Alexander and it's probable they will find an excuse to cross the Danube once again."

"I hope to God they will!" exclaimed the Turk, raising his eyes to heaven.

After some further comforting assurances I bade a cordial farewell to Moskov Selim and departed from Kaynardja in pensive mood. A curious psychological trauma, I said to myself, has occurred in this man, whose trials and tribulations surpass any previously known account of the resignation and endurance of Turkish soldiers. By nature noble and contemplative, but cruelly misunderstood by his father, he had been thrown into battle as soon as he entered manhood, unmindful not only of his womanly upbringing in the harem but also of his unfortunate mother, who loved him with such tenderness that she was unable to go on living after his sudden departure. It is strange how parents can be so deceived as to their children's thoughts and feelings. Fixing their attention on external similarities alone, both of Selim's parents judged him according to their preconceptions: in this way the father, in particular, brought about the utter ruin of his household. Truth to tell, Selim combined in his own person all the good qualities that were apportioned between the personalities of his parents: for what else were his intrepid and manly character, his pride and his sense of honour but his father's virtues? But whereas these virtues were corrupted in the old man's soul by a certain roughness of spirit, an inhuman harshness and a thoughtless severity, Selim, having inherited, besides those virtues, a gentle manner, a natural good sense, patience and kindheartedness, became a personality that commanded esteem and respect.

It seemed to me a comic caprice of nature that the gallant and warlike Selim had inherited from his mild and peaceable mother not only her, in some respects, laudable sensibility, but a wonderful liveliness of imagination that enhanced it. Selim had created a Russian life for himself in that Greek land because his vivid imagination, kindled by his weakness for the Russians, so supplemented the deficiencies of that life that what appeared comic and ridiculous to others was hidden from his sight, just as the good *hanum*, by dressing the very masculine Selim as a girl and painting his face, had created a daughter for herself in her imagination.

Thus I spent my whole journey tracing one by one in Selim's character the psychological traits which had pre-existed separately in the contradictory natures of his parents. It was evident to me that nationalism and religious fanaticism had not been expunged without trace from the consciousness of one born to such parents, but had rather been transformed into diametrically opposite convictions. After all the sacrifices he had made on behalf of the leader of his nation and religion and the psychological traumas he had suffered at the hands of his own people in recompense for those same superhuman sacrifices, any moral obligation towards them on my friend's part seemed to me to have been fulfilled once and for all. Then I began to ponder on something else.

I have often heard it said by our people that the Turks never considered the European possessions of the Ottoman state as truly belonging to them. On the contrary, they believe and profess that their natural homeland is the "Red Apple-Tree" and that, when the time comes, they will all take their women and children and will quietly and placidly cross the Bosporus, devoutly returning the keys of Byzantium to us as a sacred pledge. It is true that against this truly Byzantine hope history arrays a long series of manifestly superhuman, desperate and ferocious struggles through which, step by step, during every invasion or revolt, the Turks have sought to preserve the integrity of their Empire in Europe. But, as Selim himself suggested, what had been gained by so many victories and so many heroic feats on the part of the Turkish forces? Ever since the iron hand of the Greek revolution had shaken the Sultan's European empire, breaches had appeared in it that could no longer be dammed or repaired even with the copious blood or the innumerable bodies willingly supplied for this purpose by the faithful.

Montenegro, Serbia, Romania, even Bulgaria itself, Bosnia and Herzegovina have all fallen one after the other. Almost everywhere the plucky Turks have fought victoriously, subjugating and conquering these lands once again, and yet they have always seen themselves ejected from their own possessions through the intervention of Europe, and especially Russia.

Is it to be wondered, then, that a man such as Moskov Selim should feel that the fated hour has now come when the Caliph must transfer his throne to Damascus or Baghdad?

When, last September, I returned from the capital to the subdistrict of V., the Russian-engineered *coup d'état* to dethrone Prince Alexander of Battenberg had already taken place in Bulgaria. As soon as I arrived, a crowd gathered at my lodgings to hear the news from the European newspapers, which they supposed I had read, since the publication of such news in the local press was prohibited. Among those who came was the local medical officer, a gaunt young man with a doctorate from the University of Athens and an insatiable appetite for political discussion. When I told him Selim's story, before I left for the capital, he had exclaimed in his usual lively manner:

"They're all demoralized, all of them. Their associating with foreigners has taken away their fanaticism.

At the next setback they'll all act like Selim. None of them will obey the Sultan, and they'll all go over to the enemy."

Now, seeing the doctor again after the events in Bulgaria, I said:

"Tomorrow I'll treat you to a coffee by the waters of our local Castalian spring."

"Who'll make it for us?" he asked with a puzzled look.

"Moskov Selim, of course. I can't believe he's already left for Russia: he can't afford the fare and they won't bring him a litter, so he's waiting for me to bring news of the Russians' arrival. He'll have to wait a long time!"

"Oh, the poor man," said the doctor compassionately. "Some stupid people have brought him to death's door."

"What?" I exclaimed.

"As soon as the news came of the *coup d'état* in Bulgaria, they went and told him the Russians had come. Next day I was sent to visit him and I found him half-paralysed! He'd had a stroke, obviously brought on by his great joy."

On the following day, a little late, we went to visit him. We found him lying in his dark house on a worn reed mat. His kind face had become almost unrecognizable. His pale flesh looked more puffy and flaccid than usual. His features were drawn into a fierce scowl, which became all the more perceptible because of the rightward slant of his mouth and of one of his large eyes. He could scarcely move his arm and his right leg, the doctor informed me; but, having examined him, the doctor was convinced that the disability would pass this time, so much improved did he find the patient's condition.

"What's wrong with you, my good friend?" I asked him. "God grant you a speedy recovery!"

Until that moment Selim had not uttered a word. My heart sank when I heard his feeble, whimpering voice, which sounded as though it were emerging from a tomb.

"Thanks be to God!" said the poor man with a groan. "You can see what's wrong."

"It's nothing," I told him. "The Doctor Effendi assures me the crisis is over and you'll be well soon. But how did this terrible thing happen to you? How could you harm yourself like this? Is it worth getting so excited about nothing? The doctor tells me it was your joy that brought it on."

"Don't say that," whimpered the patient with a gesture of reproach. "If only it had been joy! God has written that I should die of sorrow! You know, I thought I would be happy too, but it wasn't to be."

Mustering his feeble energies, the Turk continued speaking in his fitful, whimpering voice, his poignantly melancholy eyes fixed on mine.

"My father and mother were Muslims. Along with all the Ottomans, I am the Sultan's property. Can a leopard change its spots? How can I deny my own blood? Betray my master? Join the Russians? That awful idea tormented me all night. All night long, my mind wrestled with my heart. At daybreak, what with my sorrow and my pondering, it just happened."

The doctor's surprised gaze met mine: I was no less surprised. When Selim had regained some strength, I said:

"But why did you need to do so much pondering? What business is all that of yours?"

"The Russians have come to Bulgaria again," said he indignantly. "Haven't you heard?"

"Oh, those villains, those liars!" I shouted. "They nearly destroyed a man's life! Didn't I promise you I would bring you the only true news? You can take it from me, my friend, that no Russian has entered, or will enter, the Sultan's domains."

"As God's your witness," he exclaimed, excitedly but painfully, "is it true they haven't come? Let me kiss you!" His eyes flashed alarmingly. "As God's your witness, will they never come again?"

Suddenly the doctor interposed himself between us, pushing me abruptly away from the patient's bedside and addressing him earnestly.

"My friend, you need to rest. Let the Russians go hang and think of your health!"

Selim began to utter some inarticulate sounds; but among them I distinctly heard the exclamation "Allah! Allah!"

When the doctor rose from the patient's pallet and turned his gaze on me, his face was as white as a sheet and his eyes were wide with horror.

"He's gone," he stammered with trembling lips. "His joy has been the death of him!"

A second seizure had put an end to the old soldier's tribulations, and… the Turk had remained a Turk.

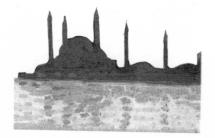

Chronological outline

1849 Born into a poor Greek family at Vizye (now Vize) in eastern Thrace (Turkey).

1850 Birth of his second sister Annio, who dies in early childhood.

1854 Death of his father, a pedlar, from typhoid. Birth of brother Michailos.

1860-67 In Constantinople, where he is apprenticed to a tailor.

1867-72 In Cyprus, where he becomes a protégé of Archbishop Sophronios. Attends school in Nicosia.

1872-73 Studies at theological seminary on the island of Chalki near Constantinople.

1873 Publishes first collection of poetry in Constantinople. Meets banker Georgios Zarifis, one of the richest Greeks in the Ottoman Empire, who enables him to complete his studies. Enters final grade of high school in Athens.

1874 In Athens, his long poem *Kodros* wins the national poetry prize and is published. Enrols as a student at Athens University.

1875   Moves to Germany, where he attends lectures at the University of Göttingen, especially those by Hermann Lotze in Medical Psychology.

1876   His collection of poems *Bosporus Breezes* wins the Greek national poetry prize.

1877   Attends courses in Classical Philology by Otto Ribbeck and in Experimental Psychology by Wilhelm Wundt at the University of Leipzig. A collection of his poems wins second prize in the national poetry competition. His elder brother Christakis is murdered.

1879   Studies at the University of Berlin.

1881   Publishes his doctoral thesis on the psychology of children's play (*Das Kinderspiel in Bezug auf Psychologie und Pädagogik*) in Leipzig.

1882-84   Makes several visits to Paris followed by an 18-month stay in London.

1883   Publishes his first short story ("My mother's sin"), first in French in Paris, then in Greek in the magazine *Estia* in Athens. Publishes two more stories in *Estia*. His poetry collection *Attic Breezes* is published (in Greek) in London at Zarifis' expense.

1884   The death of his patron Zarifis obliges him to return to live in Athens. Publishes more stories in *Estia* and elsewhere.

1885   Appointed lecturer in the history of philosophy at the University of Athens, while he also teaches psychology and logic in a high school. Publishes more stories and two books on philosophy and psychology.

1886   Continues his preparations for opening a mine in the iron-rich region of Samakovo (now Demirköy) near

Vizye, where his family owns some land. It was probably during one of his visits to the region (particularly to Kaynardja between Vizye and Saranda Ekklisies [now Kırklareli]) that he was inspired to write *Moskov Selim*.

1890   Appointed to teach at the Athens Conservatoire.

1892   Falls in love with 16-year-old Bettina Frabasile. He is confined to Dafni asylum.

1895   *Moskov Selim* is published in the newspaper *Estia*.

1896   Dies in the asylum.

MODERN
GREEK
CLASSICS

C.P. CAVAFY
Selected Poems   BILINGUAL EDITION
Translated by David Connolly

Cavafy is by far the most translated and well-known Greek
poet internationally. Whether his subject matter is historical,
philosophical or sensual, Cavafy's unique poetic voice is
always recognizable by its ironical, suave, witty and world-
weary tones.

ODYSSEUS ELYTIS
1979 NOBEL PRIZE FOR LITERATURE
**In the Name of Luminosity
and Transparency**
With an Introduction by Dimitris Daskalopoulos

The poetry of Odysseus Elytis owes as much to the ancients
and Byzantium as to the surrealists of the 1930s and the
architecture of the Cyclades, bringing romantic modernism
and structural experimentation to Greece. Collected here are
the two speeches Elytis gave on his acceptance of the 1979
Nobel Prize for Literature.

NIKOS ENGONOPOULOS
Cafés and Comets After Midnight
and Other Poems   BILINGUAL EDITION
Translated by David Connolly

Derided and maligned for his innovative and, at the time, often incomprehensible modernist experiments, Engonopoulos is today regarded as one of the most original artists of his generation and as a unique figure in Greek letters. In both his painting and poetry, he created a peculiarly Greek surrealism, a blending of the Dionysian and Apollonian.

M. KARAGATSIS
The Great Chimera
Translated by Patricia Barbeito

A psychological portrait of a young French woman, Marina, who marries a sailor and moves to the island of Syros, where she lives with her mother-in-law and becomes acquainted with the Greek way of life. Her fate grows entwined with that of the boats and when economic downturn arrives, it brings passion, life and death in its wake.

ANDREAS LASKARATOS
Reflections   BILINGUAL EDITION
Translated by Simon Darragh
With an Introduction by Yorgos Y. Alisandratos

Andreas Laskaratos was a writer and poet, a social thinker and, in many ways, a controversialist. His *Reflections* sets out, in a series of calm, clear and pithy aphorisms, his uncompromising and finely reasoned beliefs on morality, justice, personal conduct, power, tradition, religion and government.

MARGARITA LIBERAKI
The Other Alexander
Translated by Willis Barnstone and Eli Tzalopoulou Barnstone

Liberaki's allegorical novel, *The Other Alexander*, speaks to the opposing forces inherent in human nature, reenacting Greek tragedy in its evocation of a country riven by civil war and a family divided against itself. Hailed by Albert Camus as "true poetry," Liberaki's sharp, riveting prose, with its echoes of Kafka, consolidates her place in European literature.

ALEXANDROS PAPADIAMANDIS
Fey Folk
Translated by David Connolly

Alexandros Papadiamandis holds a special place in the history of Modern Greek letters, but also in the heart of the ordinary reader. *Fey Folk* follows the humble lives of quaint, simple-hearted folk living in accordance with centuries-old traditions and customs, described here with both reverence and humour.

ALEXANDROS RANGAVIS
The Notary
Translated by Simon Darragh

A mystery set on the island of Cephalonia on the eve of the Greek Revolution of 1821, this classic work of Rangavis is an iconic tale of suspense and intrigue, love and murder. *The Notary* is Modern Greek literature's contribution to the tradition of early crime fiction, alongside E.T.A. Hoffman, Edgar Allan Poe and Wilkie Collins.

EMMANUEL ROÏDES

Pope Joan

Translated by David Connolly

Roïdes' irreverent, witty and delightful novel tells the story of Joan who, according to a popular medieval legend, ascended to the Papal Throne as Pope John VIII. In Joan, Roïdes has created one of the most remarkable characters in modern Greek literature and in so doing has assured his place as one of its classic authors.

ANTONIS SAMARAKIS

The Flaw

Translated by Simon Darragh

A man is seized from his afternoon drink at the Cafe Sport by two agents of the Regime by car toward Special Branch Headquarters, and the interrogation that undoubtedly awaits him there. Part thriller and part political satire, *The Flaw* has been translated into more than thirty languages.

GEORGE SEFERIS

1963 NOBEL PRIZE FOR LITERATURE

Novel and Other Poems   BILINGUAL EDITION

Translated by Roderick Beaton

Often compared during his lifetime to T.S. Eliot, George Seferis is noted for his spare, laconic, dense and allusive verse in the Modernist idiom of the first half of the twentieth century. Seferis better than any other writer expresses the dilemma experienced by his countrymen then and now: how to be at once Greek and modern.

MAKIS TSITAS
God Is My Witness
Translated by Joshua Barley

A hilariously funny and achingly sad portrait of Greek society during the crisis years, as told by a lovable anti-hero. Fifty-year-old Chrysovalantis, who has recently lost his job and struggles with declining health, sets out to tell the story of his life, roaming the streets of Athens on Christmas Eve with nothing but a suitcase in hand.

ILIAS VENEZIS
Serenity
Translated by Joshua Barley

Inspired by the author's own experience of migration, the novel follows the journey of a group of Greek refugees from Asia Minor who settle in a village near Athens. It details the hatred of war, the love of nature that surrounds them, the hostility of their new neighbours and eventually their adaptation to a new life.

GEORGIOS VIZYENOS
Thracian Tales
Translated by Peter Mackridge

These short stories bring to life Vizyenos' native Thrace, a corner of Europe where Greece, Turkey and Bulgaria meet. Through masterful psychological portayals, each story keeps the reader in suspense to the very end: Where did Yorgis' grandfather travel on his only journey? What was Yorgis' mother's sin? Who was responsible for his brother's murder?

NIKIFOROS VRETTAKOS
Selected Poems
BILINGUAL EDITION
Translated by David Connolly

The poems of Vrettakos are firmly rooted in the Greek land-scape and coloured by the Greek light, yet their themes and sentiment are ecumenical. His poetry offers a vision of the paradise that the world could be, but it is also imbued with a deep and painful awareness of the dark abyss that the world threatens to become.

AN ANTHOLOGY
Rebetika: Songs from the Old Greek Underworld
BILINGUAL EDITION
Edited and translated by
Katharine Butterworth & Sara Schneider

The songs in this book are a sampling of the urban folk songs of Greece during the first half of the twentieth century. Often compared to American blues, rebetika songs are the creative expression of the *rebetes*, people living a marginal and often underworld existence on the fringes of established society.